Bob Moats

I0567271

Honky Tonk Murders

By Bob Moats

1

Honky Tonk Murders

For information and address:
Magic 1 Productions
P.O. Box 524, Fraser MI 48026-0524
Website: http://murdernovels.com
Cover and photo by Bob Moats

Bob Moats

Other Jim Richards series books by Bob Moats

For a preview or to purchase a book, go to
http://murdernovels.com

What a few people are saying about Murder Novels by Bob Moats

Mr. Moats, I just got your novel "Classmate Murders" and have to let you know, I read it in one evening. That is the first book I have ever done that with. That was the most enjoyable book I have ever read. I just started reading e-books, and reading again, after getting my wife a Kindle. This book was my 12th, and the best. I just got Las Vegas Showgirls to (read) tomorrow evening. I look forward to reading many of your books in this series. I have been searching for an author and books that were fun, entertaining reads. Your books are just the ticket.

Regards, A new fan, Bill from South Carolina

****

Another very nice comment submitted through my website from Micki P.:

"I recently was given a kindle for my 60th birthday. The first book I downloaded was the Classmate Murders and have now read every one of the them. Today I started on the Fatal Rejection series. Thank you for the wonderful ride with Jim and Penny and all the rest of the troop. I have laughed and giggled thru the stories, my poor family gave me the strangest looks! Now I really want a little Yorkie!! Fatal Rejection so far is another great read! I will be looking out for more of Jim Richards and since you are my #1 Author, anything of yours I can find."

Extra special thanks to:

• George "Buck" Carver, for being the inspiration for the character of Buck, and for his generous support.

• Valerie Brooks, for suggestions, checking my errors in grammar and annoying punctuation and for just being there to motivate me all the way from Florida .

• To Al Norris for beta reading and catching minor mistakes and errors.

• Special thanks to country singer Karisa Nowak for allowing me to use her in my book.

Honky Tonk Murders
by Bob Moats

Chapter 1

"She closed the door, and I just sat there,
Not moving to go and bring her back..
She had enough of my lifestyle, and I can't blame her,
I wouldn't want a man like that."

The country crooner warbled the soulful tune into the mic of the honky tonk bar just off the western edge of Las Vegas. The crowd sat and was mesmerized by his heartfelt words, then the man in the big Stetson hat stopped singing and gave a pained look, then toppled off the stage onto the front tables spilling drinks and food all over the startled customers.

Someone screamed to get a doctor, but it was too late, the country singer was dead.

Two days later on a Friday morning, I was creeping through the dark halls of the Richards Investigations and Security office. It was around five in the morning and I wanted to get in to my office

6

and do a little paperwork. No one else was in at that hour, so I was alone, I liked it that way. I entered my private domain and sat at the new desk that I had delivered last week. It was a nice mahogany and maple carved desk, with big drawers and a couple secret ones that only I knew about. I kept an extra gun in one of them.

I pulled a file and started going over it when my cell phone rang. I looked at the caller ID and saw it was Penny, my main squeeze, wife and Vegas TV talk show host.

"Hey babe what's up, I just left you at the house?" I said into the tiny hole of my cellphone and listened to the slightly bigger hole to hear her reply.

"Jim, I just got a call from my cousin, she's in need of help," Penny said sounding half-asleep.

"Your cousin calls you at five in the morning? What did she want?"

"Her husband died a couple days ago and she thinks he was murdered. She knew I was married to you and living here in Vegas and wanted to know if you could help her?"

"Well, tell her to call me when we open, I'll see what she has and go from there. Now go back to bed and meet me for lunch, just call first."

She said she would and hung up. I sat back wondering why her relative would call so early. I knew this cousin lived in Phoenix, Arizona, she was Penny's only cousin that she ever talked about. The cousin, Jenny Wayne, was married to some rising country singer that had modest record sales on the country charts. I tried to remember the singer's name, but was drawing a blank. The last name wasn't Wayne, that sounded too Yankee, so the singer took on a stage name.

I went back to my paperwork, trying get the cases that had been completed ready for Lacey to file. The last month had been busy for us; we had everything from chasing down missing grooms to foiling industrial espionage for a big pharmaceutical company.

Las Vegas was a good move for Penny and me, I felt. Back in Michigan we had many adventures starting with the infamous classmate murders. I had this strange thing about being followed by murder, and Penny loved to play up that curse. I didn't believe it, but being a private investigator, murder was bound to come up occasionally.

I heard a door open towards the front of the building. I glanced at the digital clock on my desk and it read just before six. Still too early for anyone to show up, I waited as I heard footsteps coming down the hall. I had disabled the building alarm so if it was one of my cohorts, they would know someone was in the building.

Buck suddenly appeared at my door and gave me a big smile.

"Whatcha doing in here so early Jimmy?" the big man asked.

"Paperwork, so we can get paid. What are you doing here so early, as you say?"

"Have to reschedule a few guards at one to the dealerships and call in a few to work. It's been more work than I thought there would be. Back when I was a security guard in Michigan, I used to just sit all night, no cares, now being the boss, just too much work."

"I can understand, how's business?"

"Good, we have over a hundred and sixty guards now, all spread out over Vegas, protecting properties from the bad guys," he said with a smile. "Don't work too hard, I got to make a few calls to get people out of bed to go to work. That's the part I enjoy." He went off to his office, leaving me to go back to my paperwork.

Around seven-thirty, Lacey came bouncing in and said good morning. "You're in early, good, got your end of the month reports ready for me?"

"Yes, boss, I do," I said with a smile and stood to give Lacey the files I had finished. She took them and went back to her desk up front.

I was still standing by my office door when heard her phone ring up front and then heard Lacey's voice over the intercom saying I had a call. I went back to my desk and sat, picking up the desk phone and hit the blinking button.

"Good morning, Jim Richards speaking," I said feeling more awake now.

"Jim, it's Penny's cousin Jenny, did she tell you I called?" came the voice on the phone, sounding like it came from a thirteen-year-old girl.

"Yes, Jenny, she did. You told her that you think your husband was murdered?"

"The police aren't telling me much so far, let me explain. Ricky is my husband, was, and he was in Las Vegas for the big CMA country music awards they have there every year. It's this weekend. He was performing two days ago at some little club in town and they say he just fell over and died. Jim, he was only thirty-one, a person of that age just doesn't just fall over and die. I'm in Phoenix and can't get out there to Vegas, we have a daughter in the hospital with a blood disorder and I have to be here for her. I didn't know what to do, but I remembered that Penny had moved to Vegas and you were a detective. Can you help me find out what is going on?"

"Jenny, let me make a few calls and see what I can find out. You can't come out here at all?"

"No, I'm the only family here and I have to be near my daughter. I really want to be out there but it's impossible."

"Okay, sit tight and I'll be back to you as soon as I can. Now what name did your husband go by?"

"Ricky Lawless, he thought it was a name that would get him some attention, I didn't like it but his agent and the recording company people thought it was a good hook. He was getting popular on the music charts."

"All right, I'll see what I can find out, I'll call you back later today," I said and noted the phone number off the caller ID and she thanked me.

I sat back thinking of how to attack the problem. I could call Lynn Carter and see if she has anything on it, she was homicide and may have something. I reached for my desk phone just as Trapper walked in.

"Hey Jim, what ya working on?" Trapper said then plopped down on my client chair.

"Just come in why don't you."

"Thanks, I'm already in. Got anything exciting?"

"Just finished our monthly reports and I got a call from a cousin of Penny's, seems her country singing husband was in town for the CMA country award show this weekend and he died while performing in some club a couple days ago. She can't come out so she asked me if I could help. I was just going to call Lynn Carter to see if she knows anything about it."

"Lynn is good people. Oh and Earl has flown the coop. He and Paula ran off and went up to the mountains. Seems Paula wanted to get away from all the bright lights and to shake off the big city. The media is still talking about the Elvis murders you know."

"Yeah, it was good that we caught the guy who killed the top Elvis in town and was murdering all the drug dealers. That will make a good book for later. Now do you have anything else to do besides delay me?"

"Nope, just wanted to let you know I was in the area, and will be all day."

"I'll note that in my appointment book, now beat it so I can go to work."

Trapper laughed and stood, "Someday you'll need me." Then he left.

I was laughing as I dialed Lynn Carter. She came on and I told her it was me, asked if she knew about the death of a country singer and gave her the name. She said she did and asked why I needed to know.

"He's a cousin of Penny's, the guy's wife called and wanted to see if I could help. I said I'd see what I could find out. Can you tell me what happened?

"Preliminary report says he died of a coronary attack, which was the ME's initial findings, but Joe Lang isn't so sure, no proof yet, but he's thinking it may have been murder."

*

Chapter 2

"Is Earl around, I have to ask him something?" Lynn said.

"Too late, he and Paula went out to go camping up in the mountains somewhere," he replied. "They took off without telling anyone, except Trapper."

"Probably Mt. Charleston, where we camped back during the Sin City project murders. I'll try calling him on his cell. Anything else you need to know about the country singer?"

"Yeah, can I go talk to Joe Lang about him?"

"You can visit the morgue anytime you want, preferably on a slab," she said with a big laugh.

"Thanks Lynn, I love you too. Talk later," I said and hung up.

"Everyone's a comedian," I said to myself. Lacey was at the door and asked who I was talking to.

"No one, just talking to myself. You need something from me too?"

"Nope, just bringing you the Review-Journal. You usually get the paper last and by then it's all torn apart. Since you were here early this morning I wanted to see you get it first."

"Well, that's very nice of you Lacey, thank you. I'll read it and give it back to you."

"No, just toss it on Trappers desk and run. He likes to be the first to read it, but he has a tendency of getting it out of order and cutting things out."

"What would he be cutting out?"

"Coupons, articles that he finds interesting. Just enough to make the paper useless for the next person."

"Is that why I never see it?"

"Probably. Are you going to check on the dead cowboy now?"

"How did you know about that?"

"The woman who called identified herself and started to tell me about it, I just told her to talk to you. Plus, it's in the paper, so you can read about it. Section C, entertainment."

"Thank you," I said as Lacey left the room.

I laid out the paper on my desk. I hardly ever read it in the office and at home Penny usually had it spread out in the kitchen for our toy Yorkie, Willy. As much as I loved the dog, I'd rather have a ferret or a de-scented skunk. I guess I was a little odd like that. Willy was our baby now, so Penny had to see that when we left him home alone, he didn't do his business on the kitchen floor, so I rarely got to read the paper.

I found the entertainment section and flipped the pages until I found the small article on the death of the country singer.

Honky Tonk Murders

The article gave the standard denials that the police give reporters to cover the facts. I could read between the lines but there was not much here to read. The singer had an attack on stage and toppled into the audience. That was all there was about his death. He wasn't up for any awards in the big yearly country music show, but showing up was good for his image. He could hob-nob with all the biggies of country and maybe get an endorsement that his record label could use. Poor guy, I thought, so close.

Then I thought about Penny's cousin out in Phoenix, stuck with a sick child while her husband's body was back here on a slab in the morgue. I'd have to see what could be done to get the body back to her.

I finished the paper and then just for fun, started to rearrange the pages out of order. I stood and took the thing to Trapper's office and dropped it on his desk.

"Aren't you a little old to be a paperboy?" Trapper asked as he eyed the paper.

"Enjoy yourself," was all I said as I left the room.

I went back to my office and gathered the things I would need and went to the front to tell Lacey that I was going out.

"Where are you going to just in case anyone asks?" Lacey said.

"The morgue, for my annual health check-up," I said with a smirk and went out the front door.

I had only been to the Clark County morgue a couple times since I had been out in Vegas. It wasn't my favorite place to visit, but a necessity to help with cases. I remembered back to the mortuary murders and the bodies spread out there, not a pleasant memory, the Clark County morgue wasn't much better.

I drove into the parking lot of the building housing the morgue, went in to the front desk and asked to see Joe Lang. The big cop got on the phone and called ahead. Joe granted me a pass to get in and I found the medical examiner trying to crack the ribs of a rather dingy looking male body.

"Don't you just love the smell of guts in the morning, it smells like murder," I said with a smile.

Joe was silently laughing causing his body to pulse. "A homeless person found dead this morning on Tropicana, sad. What brings you here on a beautiful morning, when you should be out chasing criminals or women?"

"Penny would have me on this table if I chased women. I'm on a case of the death of one of Penny's cousins. What do you know about Ricky Lawless?"

"Number 23 with a bullet," Joe said.

"He was shot?" I asked in surprise.

"You don't follow music do you?"

"No, I have an MP3 player that Penny puts stuff on, most of it is good, newer stuff like New Kids on the Block."

Joe stopped cracking the ribs and stared at me. "Boy you don't know music. No Jim, 'with a bullet' is a term meaning a recording by a singer is moving up the charts fast. Lawless had a couple good records out and they were doing well on the country music charts."

"Okay, that still means little to me; I don't listen to or care for country music. Well that's not totally true,

I like Shania Twain, Faith Hill and Sugarland. Do they count?"

"Yes Jim, they do count. Now Lawless was a new crossover country performer, which means his music could be enjoyed by both country and popular music listeners. He was brought in the morgue and I performed the autopsy, finding nothing extraordinary but it looked like heart failure. I'm still waiting for the tox report to see if he had anything in his system that may have caused his heart to burst. We're so backed up I'll be surprised if I get word by next week. Are you going to claim the body for Penny's cousin?"

"I hadn't thought about it, his wife can't come to get him, she's nursing a sick daughter in the hospital and can't leave Phoenix."

"Well then, you may have to take the body to her. Since Penny is a legal relative, she would have to sign a few papers and then you can claim his remains."

I hadn't thought about taking the body to Jenny, but there weren't many other options. "I guess so, let me talk to Penny and her cousin to see how they want to handle it. Can you get me word if you find anything hinkey in the tox?"

"If I find anything hinkey, I'll let you know. Give me a couple days to finish processing the body."

"You got it, I'm in no rush to put a body in my back seat and drive him home."

Joe was laughing silently again, "There are procedures for that, I'll fill you in when you are ready."

"Thanks Joe, keep me informed," I said as I went

out of the cutting room and taking a big clean breath outside of the building. I had seen a good number of dead bodies in my career, even made a few myself, but it always affected me.

I drove back towards the office but called Penny to see if she wanted to go to lunch earlier than we originally planned. She said she was ready, so I changed directions and drove back to the house and picked up my favorite girl.

"What did you do with the dog?" I asked when she got in the car.

"I put him in the kitchen and blocked the door. I hope he stays in there. I think Willy is rebelling when we leave him alone."

"Well, we could have taken him with us, you know you'll have to clean up the poop or the food dragged all over the floor."

"I thought I could be stronger with the poop, but I won't give in. I accept it, he's such a cute dog."

"He's not a dog, he's a dish rag with ears. Being a toy Yorkie, he's so small he shouldn't get into much trouble. It's like having a gerbil. You could look into one of those if you get tired of Willy."

"No way I could ever get rid of him. Where are we going to eat?"

"I was thinking Arturo's, I could use some good pasta. We also need to talk about your cousin's body. And what we are going to do about it."

"Can we talk about that after we eat? It's not conversation for food."

"Agreed, I just came from the morgue and I'm not wanting to think about it while I eat. Crap," I suddenly said.

"What?"

"Pasta resembles intestines; I don't think I want pasta now."

"Okay, I'd settle for burgers, does that offend your senses?"

"Sonic it is." I steered the car in the direction of the nearest Sonic Burger, pulled into a parking slot and ordered through the remote box. I liked Sonic, the waitresses on roller skates took me back to my younger days when they had lots of carhops. We got our food and ate, then putting the remains back in the tray hooked to the door, waiting for the carhop to come get it.

"Now shall we discuss about getting your cousin's hubby back to Phoenix?"

*

Chapter 3

"So there's no word about his death, other than heart failure?" Penny asked.

"Not according to Joe Lang, yet. He's waiting for more results. I'd like to know if this is murder or not. I don't want to have to chase down false leads if he wasn't taken out."

"Sweetie, I know you, you're still going to investigate it," Penny said with a smile and stroked my head. I loved when she did that and we usually ended up in bed. We were still out in public so that option was not immediately on the table.

"Can you call your cousin and tell her to make arrangements for the funeral home and burial? Oh and ask if Ricky had life insurance."

"I'll do that when I get home. Now what are we going to do?"

"Feel like visiting the office?"

"Sure, I haven't been there since last week."

I waited until the girl on skates had taken the tray from the car and rolled off to the building. I pulled out and drove back.

We were coming down the hallway from the back entrance when Lacey came from the front.

"Jim, you got a call from Joe Lang, he needs to talk to you. I was just going to call you but I saw on the spy camera that you were coming in the building."

I thanked her and smiled about the reference to the spy camera. When we first moved into the new building, I found that all the offices, lobby and both front and back doors had security cameras on them. They all fed into a small room in the back where there were monitors and recorders. Hey, this is Vegas, where they have video watching your every move. Lacey also had monitors at her desk so she could keep an eye on the comings and goings of people.

"Thanks Lacey, I'll call," I said, then Penny kissed and thanked me for lunch, then went off with Lacey to discuss women things, I figured.

Honky Tonk Murders

I went into my office and sat, picking up the phone I thumbed through the contact list in the book I kept on the desk and found Joe's number. I was waiting for Joe to come on and then he answered.

"Joe, it's Jim, you have something so soon?"

"Just after you left I got a call from a friend in tox and he said that he personally processed Ricky Lawless because he was a country music fan and he found high levels of muriate of potash AKA potassium chloride. High enough dosage to cause heart failure. I'm calling this a homicide unless Ricky committed suicide by ingesting it."

"The guy had too much to live for, I doubt he would kill himself," I said thinking about this new info. "Where does one get potassium chloride?"

"It's not sold in the local grocery store in it's pure form, but it can be bought. Potassium chloride makes up 70% of Ace Hardware's vegetation-friendly "Ice Melt", though it's inferior in ice melting quality to calcium chloride. It's also used in fertilizer and mixed with table salt in small dosages. Potassium chloride is used as a third of a three-drug combination in lethal injection for death row criminals. Lots of uses and the worst is death."

"Did CSI investigate the scene when he died for anything he could have ingested it from?"

"Yep, and I checked while waiting for you to call, they found no glass he could have been drinking from near the body. Either someone took it after he crashed or he drank the liquid before the show."

"I may need to take a look at that club and see what I can find. Thanks Joe. Have you informed Lynn about this?"

"Of course, it's her case, and she stays around where I can reach her."

"I'll give you my cell phone number next time," I said with a laugh and hung up. I sat back in my chair and thought about the next move. Time to go boot-scootin and have a look at the club where Rick sang his last song.

I found Penny and Lacey watching the huge LCD TV in the lobby, and since Penny was taking a few days off from her show, it was a rerun of her talk show with guest, Julio Iglesias. The man may be getting older, but he still had the look. Penny reached her hand out to me and pulled me to the couch where she and Lacey were sitting on.

"What's the word, Sweetie?" she asked.

"Joe says it's murder, so I'm on the case. I'll call Jenny and break the news to her then you two can talk about transporting the body back and funeral arrangements. If we have to, we can take Ricky's body back to Jenny if it will save a few dollars for her. I'm sure a funeral parlor would charge a fortune to bring him home. We'll make sure to find out about insurance, and if his recording company had a policy on him. They'd be crazy not to if his records were climbing the charts."

"We can call her from home," Penny said, half of her attention to me and the other half to Julio. I tilted my head around Penny's and smiled. She told me to move and I did, up and back to my office.

Honky Tonk Murders

I pulled my desk phone closer and dialed Lynn, waited as she answered.

"Jim I was going to call you. You said Ricky Lawless was Penny's cousin?"

"Yep, he was and I talked to Joe Lang already"

"Joe told me he did, is Penny going to arrange to have the body taken back to his wife?"

"We talked about it, I have to call her first to break the news about how he died. I remember Trapper telling me the worst thing a cop would have to do was to tell a family that a loved one was murdered. Natural causes was bad enough but murder... not good."

"I hear you. So you guys are going to take the body?"

"So far, yes, why?"

"Since the man was poisoned, we may need to do further tests, just to be sure."

"Doesn't the tox prove this?"

"It does but we need to be sure. Just a formality. As soon as more samples are taken, we'll release the body to you. Make arrangements with the morgue for the transfer permit then you can take him."

"Will do. Now was there anything from the crime scene that can corroborate the cause of death?"

"Corroborate? Now you are sounding like a TV detective, no, CSI hasn't came up with anything to connect to his murder. Are you going to be investigating now?"

"The wife asked me to look into it, I won't step on your toes, but we can share info as we get it, if that is good for you?"

"Sure, it's good to have a second opinion on cases, I'll let you know if we come up with anything, and you do likewise."

"Yep, so I have to go call the grieving widow, I'll talk to you later." I hung up and looked to Penny now standing in the doorway to my office.

"Shall we go call Jenny?" I said.

"Let's call from here, I don't want to go see the damage the dog has done on our home yet."

"Sure, let him totally destroy the place before we get there. Okay, close the door and I'll call her."

Penny closed the door and sat in the client chair next to the desk. I hit the intercom button and told Lacey that I didn't want to be disturbed for at least a half hour. She agreed and I picked up my phone again, dialing the number I had written on the pad of paper from my caller ID of Jenny's phone call.

The phone rang about four times before Jenny answered. "Hello?"

"Jenny, this is Jim, I have some bad news," I said to prepare her for the worse. "The coroner's report is going to say that it was a homicide. He was poisoned. That's all they have for now, they're still going to be running some tests and then we can bring Ricky home. Do you have a funeral parlor in town that you can make arrangements with?"

She was silent for a bit too long, I figured she was composing herself. Maybe I could have been a little less brisk about it, but she needed to be told the worse.

"There is one parlor I have been to for a friend's funeral, I'll call them. When will Ricky be coming home?"

"I'm not sure, but tell the funeral home that we will be bringing him out, so they don't have to charge you for that. Did Ricky have a life insurance policy?"

"He did, I'll call the insurance man and tell him about this."

"Since Ricky was murdered, the policy may have a double indemnity clause for benefits, not trying to take advantage of the situation, but every dollar counts now. Did Ricky's recording label have a policy on him or any death benefits for survivors?"

"I don't know about that, I haven't even heard from his agent or the label people, they haven't called about his death, I'm not happy."

"Do you know if Ricky's portion of the royalties from his songs will go to you now?"

"Jim, I'm not very good with all that stuff, I'm just trying to be with my daughter and keep my head above water."

"Okay, don't worry, Penny and I will help you to get through this, just be patient and I'll let you know what's happening." She thanked me and we finished the call.

I turned to Penny and said, "I'm seeing a big mystery coming."

*

Chapter 4

"We can't take the body until they release it, so the investigation goes on. That gives me time to check out the club where he died. You want to continue watching TV with Lacey or go with me?"

"Sweetie, I prefer you, Lacey is cute but, well you're cuter," she said with a smile. "Let me get my things."

I told Lacey that we would be at the bar where Ricky Lawless died and to hold my calls.

"You don't get that many calls to worry about it," Lacey said with a smirk.

"Just take messages and be nice."

Penny came up as I was calling Lynn to get the name of the club where Ricky expired.

"It's called Shindigs and it's over on Rainbow Boulevard, east side, one block south of Tropicana. We already talked to everyone there; do you think you can get better intel?" Lynn asked.

"I'm sure I can beat the truth out of a few waitresses. If you look away."

"I'll do that if you get a suspect for me."

"I'll try my best, thanks Lynn." I hung up and put the phone in my pocket.

Penny asked if I was ready to go country, I laughed and said, "Sho'nuff, cowgirl."

We drove out Tropicana and down Rainbow into the parking lot of the bar. There weren't very many cars in the lot, it was well after noon, so the lunch crowd probably had left, even if they served a lunch. What would they serve, buffalo burgers, rib of cow with beans? Didn't sound appetizing. I parked and we went in the front door that had some kind of bullhorn for a door handle, it was well used.

The place was dark at first until our eyes adjusted, then it was just strange. To the right was a very long bar, from almost the front of the building to just past half way down the room. There had to be every kind of liqueur and beer available in the world on the back bar. I guess cowboys love their drinks. There were two cowgirls behind the bar wearing off the shoulder frilly blouses and tight white shorts, which showed a lot of butt cheeks. I guess cowboys love their women in skimpy clothes.

All over the middle of the room were four-top tables and along the left wall were longer banquet type tables for the ranch hands I presumed. Behind the long tables were framed posters on the walls of every beer available. Way to the back of the room was a stage, built up about a foot off the ample dance floor in front of it. On the stage were tons of amps, speakers, microphones and a steel guitar. There were guitars on stands waiting for their masters to stroke them into music. The banner on the wall behind the band equipment said, "Nashland Band". There were two waitresses walking the floor cleaning the tables of plates and drinks left by people who had lunch and left.

Penny and I went to the bar where I sat us next to the wait station. It was the small space at the bar with rails where the waitresses would order drinks for the patrons. Whenever I was in a bar, I usually sat by the station so I could talk to the waitresses while they waited for their drink orders.

The busty blonde behind the bar asked what would be our pleasure, Penny whispered in my ear to be careful what I said. I smiled and said a draft, Penny requested a wine spritzer. The waitress looked at Penny like she was from another planet, so Penny changed it to a Jack red on the rocks. That got a better response; she went off to fill our order as I surveyed the room.

One of the waitresses came up to the station with an armful of plates and glasses on a tray. She plopped it on the bar and started to take the glasses off placing them on another tray for washing. I smiled and she gave me a big smile back. Penny poked me in the back.

I turned and said, "I can leave you home while I investigate. I'm just being friendly to get them to talk, okay?"

She gave me a smirk and said, "Do your thing, Mickey Spillane."

I turned back to the girl and asked, "Excuse me, were you here the night that Ricky Lawless died?

"No, I was off that night, but Linda was here," she said pointing to a brunette walking towards the bar with a tray of glasses. She went off and I waited for Linda to bring her tray up.

She came up and gave me a smile, I asked again, "Hi, can you tell me if you were here the night Ricky Lawless died?"

Honky Tonk Murders

Her smile dissolved and she looked sad now. "Yes, I was here. I was standing on the sidewall watching Ricky sing when he suddenly fell down and died. It was tragic. I couldn't believe he was gone. He said he was going to marry me when his record went up to the top ten."

I glanced to Penny who had a surprised look on her face, probably the same look I had. "Ricky was going to marry you?"

"Yes he was, as soon as he divorced his wife, Mary Lou. She lives in LA and he had started divorce proceedings on her."

"He told you he had a wife in LA? Did he ever mention a wife in Arizona?"

"Arizona? No, he never mentioned that his wife was from Arizona. Should this be something I would know?"

"Well, his wife is in Arizona, his real wife. He told you she was in LA, right?"

"Yeah he did. She wasn't?"

"Well, the wife we know lives in Arizona. This is news to me. What else did he tell you?"

"He never said he lived in Arizona, he said he was from Nashville, and moved to LA when he got married to Mary Lou. They had a home near Echo Park. She even came in here one night, I didn't say anything, I just held back while he dealt with the psycho bitch."

"She was a psycho bitch, why?"

"She was screaming about how he was spending the money from his records for things he didn't need."

"Did she say what kind of things?"

"Clothes, drugs, anything that he liked, she didn't approve."

"How did she happen to be here, did he bring her or did she arrive by herself?"

"That I couldn't tell you, she came in about a week ago when he was working and started on my, screaming about this and that. I felt sorry for him. Listen, I have to finish my tables," she said looking antsy.

I gave her a twenty and thanked her. She went off to finish her section. I turned to Penny, "Well, this is interesting. We need to find this Mary Lou wife and find out what the deal is. I'll call Lynn and see if she can get into her system to track a motel where this woman could be. If Ricky registered under his stage name."

"I'm afraid to call Jenny and tell her about this," Penny said.

"No, don't bring it up until we find out what's going on."

We sat slowly sipping on our drinks, it was too early for me to drink beer, but this was acceptable for now. It was difficult for me to be in a bar without a beer in hand.

Linda came back up to us and stood, I turned, smiled again and asked, "What's on your mind?"

"You said he had a wife in Arizona?"

"Yes he did, my wife is a cousin. I'm sorry, this is my wife, Penny Wickens. It's her cousin who was married to Ricky."

Linda's eyes went a bit larger when she realized who Penny was. "Oh wow, you're the Vegas Alive host?"

Penny smiled and took her hand that the now excited waitress held out. "Yes, I am, and my cousin Jenny said she was married to Ricky. But now you say he was married to some woman in Los Angeles. We're investigating his death, is there anything you may know that can help us?"

The woman looked to me, then I could see the recognition in her eyes, "You're Jim Richards, the P.I. aren't you. I've read about you in the RJ."

"Well, the Review-Journal has been kind to me. Do you know if Ricky had anyone mad at him other than his LA wife?"

"No, everyone loved Ricky, he was kind and gentle, a real person. He wrote great music, which was going to make him rich when the records took off. Now it doesn't matter."

"Has this LA wife been in here since his death?"

"No, she just disappeared after that."

"What were Ricky's habits, did he drink heavily? Did he drink anything the night he died?"

"Ricky never drank alcohol, he only drink soda. He always drank a glass of water before he would get up to sing, to clear his throat he said."

"The night he died, did he have a glass of water and where did he get it from? I mean did he get it himself or did someone bring it to him?"

"I brought him the glass; I got the water from the tap on the bar. He drank a little to clear his throat then put the glass on his stool behind him. He would drink from it after every song to moisten his throat or so he would say."

"I don't suppose you saw anyone go near his drink?"

"I wasn't really watching the glass, just Ricky and the crowd. He had a good following building up here."

"How long was he performing here?"

"Three weeks up to the CMA show, then he was going back to LA he said. I don't know what I'm going to do without him."

I turned to Penny and said quietly, "Neither will his wife."

*

Chapter 5

Penny took a sip of her drink and made a face. I smiled and said, "You don't care for whiskey, why'd you order it?"

"I didn't want to look like a wuss to the bartender. I just ordered something I heard on an old movie," she said with a smile.

I kissed her cheek and said, "You are something, I guess I'll keep you."

I turned back to Linda, "How did Ricky get around, did he have a car?"

"No, he had a Chevy pick-up. A big S-20 that he loved."

I looked to Penny again, "Pick-up truck, part of the country dream." I turned back to Linda and asked, "Where is his pick-up now?"

She looked a little puzzled, "I'm not sure, last I saw it was in the parking lot when he arrived the night he died, I didn't look for it afterwards."

"Where was it parked on that night?"

"In the back. I don't think the police ever asked about it. It should still be there unless someone took it."

"Thanks Linda, we'll check it." I gave her another twenty, she thanked me and went off. I turned to Penny and said, "Shall we go break into a pick-up?"

"Anything's better than this drink."

I laughed and stood. "Shall we go boot-scootin out the back way?"

We went through the door going out to the back parking lot. It was dirt and gravel, with a large empty field behind the lot. Weeds had grown up hiding the back forty probably needing to be plowed.

I looked around at the few cars probably owned by the employees and spotted a pick-up truck with Arizona plates.

"I guess Linda didn't check out his plates. But this doesn't explain the LA wife if he's driving an Arizona truck. I really hate mystery."

"That's a fine thing to say for a P.I., even if you aren't the best one in the world."

"Thank you, I happen to be a very good investigator, just ask any of my loyal fans."

"All three of them," she said with a smirk. We went to the truck and luckily it wasn't locked up.

"I guess country folk trust people," I said as I opened the driver's door. "I'm really surprised that Lynn didn't find this truck. Of course she has been a bit distracted lately. She and Deacon are not having a good relationship at the moment; I think they both are suffering for it. We need to have an intervention for them."

"Sounds good to me, if they fail in their relationship where is there hope for the world?" Penny said.

"The world will have to use us as a shining example," I said with a short laugh.

"It helps that we don't have to put up with each other all day long, like Lynn and Deacon do. They need to separate their jobs."

"I mentioned that to Deacon a while back, he agreed. Now let's see what we have here." I looked into the truck and it was a mess. Papers everywhere, soda pop cans and a few beer cans strewn around the cab. I opened the glove box and found a plastic bag with some white powder, I deduced it to be some drug. Penny snorted and said, "Brilliant Holmes."

I pulled my cell phone and speed dialed Lynn. She came on after a few rings, "Jim, got me a killer?"

"No, but I got some info for you. Can you meet me in the back parking lot of Shindigs?"

She pulled in about twenty minutes later as Penny and I sat on the tailgate of the truck waiting.

"Where's Deacon?" I asked.

"We've separated," she said nonchalantly.

Penny sucked air and said, "I'm so sorry."

"No, it's good, we are still together but we've just

gone different direction in the job. Deacon is now in vice, even though I'm not happy about it, but we needed to get away from each other on the job. It's too hard to have to bring home our work when we are on the same cases. We got to arguing too much about our opinions of the case."

"I'm glad you are at least hanging in at home," I said.

"Are you kidding, we're joined at the hip when it comes to relationships. Just needed to separate our professional lives. Now what do you have?"

I pointed to the truck, "It's Ricky Lawless' truck, and he supposedly has a second wife in LA. Can you do the search to find her?"

"I'll try, I just need some background."

I explained everything that Linda had told us, Lynn was smiling all the while I related my story.

"What's so funny?" I asked.

"It just sounds like a country song, pick-up truck, two women, and a honky tonk bar. I wonder where the dog is?"

Penny and I both got a laugh out of that and Lynn got on her cell to call CSI in to check the truck. "I screwed up by not asking about this vehicle. Thanks for that. The bag looks like drugs, I hope for your cousin's sake he wasn't dealing."

"It's bad enough that he may have been a bigamist, drug dealing would be a step up," Penny said. I had to agree.

Two techs from CSI showed up about twenty minutes later and the three of us went back into the bar. Lynn flashed her badge and said to Linda that she was going off duty until they could hash over a few details. Linda looked to the manager who was out from his office now and he had to agree to let Lynn talk to her. We all went to a table up front by the large windows that let the afternoon sunshine shine in.

"Linda, I'm sorry if I was brisk with you this last week, but I had a lot on my plate, now can you relate everything that happened again that night lawless died."

Linda pretty much told her the same as she told us earlier, Lynn looked to Penny when Linda mentioned about the LA wife. Lynn thanked her and she went off.

"So Penny, your cousin says Ricky was her husband?"

"This is nothing new, Jenny and I talked about it a couple years back when his recordings were being made, nothing big yet, he was just starting. So I knew that he was married to Jenny. But who's to say he didn't have a wife in LA too?"

"I'll check on it and see what I can find." Lynn called Linda back over, she came right away. "Did you get a name of this wife from LA?"

"I heard Ricky call her Mary Lou one time, that's all I know. She's probably Mary Lou Lawless," Linda said.

"Ricky's last name wasn't Lawless, it was Wayne. He used a stage name," I said.

"Well, I don't know about that. I never heard her last name mentioned."

Lynn thanked her and she went off again, "I'll

check on both Mary Lou Lawless and Mary Lou Wayne to see what pops," she said to us. Lynn gave us a big smile and said, "I'll be back at the precinct, call if anything new develops." She went out to her car and drove away.

Penny and I went back to sit at the bar and ordered another drink, we both needed it. There was a show on the TV about the CMA award show coming up at the MGM Grand concert hall. We sat watching as I looked down the bar to see a woman in an animated conversation with the barmaid. Linda was standing nearby and then came down to us hurriedly.

"Mr. Richards, we got a problem, that woman at the bar claims to be Ricky's wife; she wants to know what happened."

I guess I had the same surprised look that Penny had and told Linda to have the woman come to us. She went to the agitated woman and said something to her, pointing to us. The woman came down the bar and up to Penny and me.

I said as she stood next to me, "Hi, I'm Jim and this is my wife Penny. She happens to be Ricky's cousin, did he mention her to you at all?"

The woman looked a little surprised at the news and was silent for a beat. "No, he never mentioned her, but we weren't married that long for him to open up about his family. Good to meet you. Do you know what happened to him?"

"How did you find out he was dead?" I asked.

She was silent again, as if she was trying to get her facts straight. "I called here yesterday and was told he died this last week, I had to come and find out what happened, do you know?"

"How long have you been married to Ricky and where are you from?"

"Shouldn't I be the one asking the questions?"

"Well, you can answer my questions or you can answer Vegas homicide's questions. They just left here, now who are you?"

She looked to Penny, "Are you really his cousin?"

"According to Ricky's real wife I am, now answer my husband's question, who are you?"

She looked a little shook, but kept her composure. She reached back and took out a wallet and opened it to reveal an ID stating she was an investigator of the Western Life Insurance Company.

"Now who are you?" she said to me.

I pulled my ID and showed her. "I'm owner of Richards Investigations, my wife is actually Ricky's cousin and his wife asked me to investigate his death. You were sent here by the insurance company?"

She gave me a slight smile and said, "Looks like we are on the same side."

*

Chapter 6

Penny mumbled, "Don't go taking sides yet." Not loud enough for anyone to hear but me, I just gave her my look.

"So you're an insurance investigator?" I asked trying to ignore Penny's comments.

"Yes, I've been with the company for about two years. It's an interesting job, finding people who try to cheat the system and I save the company money."

"Do they give you a bounty for cheats found?"

"I wish. No, I get paid a salary, but the perks are good, they pay for my travel and lodging, I get to choose which hotels to stay in. Vegas is a treat for me."

"Oh, I'm Jim Richards and this is my wife…"

"Penny Wickens, I used to watch your talk show on the CW while I traveled the country living in the occasional lousy motel. Sorry I didn't mean to interrupt, nice to meet both of you. I'm Buffy McCabe."

"Buffy the cheat slayer?" I said.

She laughed and said, "Thanks, I've heard worse. I'm the only female investigator in the company, so I have to try harder, and having a name like Buffy doesn't help."

"Why don't you use an alias?"

"I would have, but my bosses didn't give me a chance. I think they want me to fail, this is my sixth case and I haven't proven much and this case could help."

"So why are you investigating Ricky and why pretend to be his wife, isn't that a little risky?"

"I knew his first wife was not with him, the one in Arizona, now the one from LA, that's another matter. I was trying to shake up the LA wife into doing something stupid, so if I claimed to be his wife she may tip her hand as to why she is here. As for why I'm investigating Ricky, he had a three million dollar policy with us, and with double indemnity, his wife is a rich woman. The real one at least. We want to be sure the second one doesn't try to claim the cash. And find out how he actually died so we can determine the proper payout or if anyone even deserves the money."

"How did you know about the LA wife?"

"I've been on this for two days, I keep my eyes and ears open. I have an assistant in LA hunting up a marriage license on the second wife. I don't know how bigamy will affect the policy, but the Arizona wife is listed as beneficiary. The LA wife could cause trouble."

"Six million dollars, that's a good cause for murder," I said.

"If the first wife didn't do it, which would nullify the policy in her favor. The second wife doing the deed would just be a cause for putting her away for good. Now do you have anything to share with me?"

"No more than you already mentioned. Did you know he was poisoned?"

"I kind of figured that, but how is the question."

"He ingested the poison; we just need to figure out when he drank the fatal drink. Linda, who gave him a glass of water that night, says she was supposed to get married to Ricky, when he divorced his LA wife. She didn't know about the Arizona wife. If the LA wife knew this, then she may have felt threatened enough to murder him. Either way, Linda wouldn't have benefited from his death."

"Unless she was mad enough if she found out that he was married to two woman, if she knew." Buffy turned to look at Linda, "She doesn't look the type to commit murder but I've seen meeker murderers."

As we sat talking, the stage was being populated by band members, getting their amps turned on and their guitars tuned. I hadn't realized it was getting so late. I turned to Penny and said, "Shall we hang around to listen to the band?"

"Sho'nuff cowboy," she said with a smile.

My cell phone buzzed and the ID said it was Trapper. "Yes, Mr. Trapper, what can I do for you?"

"Just seeing how you're doing on your country case?"

"I'm finding all kinds of lyrics for a good country tune, why?"

"I'm just bored, where are you at?"

"The country bar where Ricky was murdered. Penny and I are sitting here with a lady investigator for Ricky's life insurance company, just waiting for the band to start."

"I'll be there in twenty minutes," he said and hung up. I wondered if he knew where we were, but Trapper is resourceful. I put my cell phone away as Linda came up and stood in front of Buffy looking like she wanted answers.

"Who are you and why are you saying you were married to Ricky?" she demanded. I had to stifle a laugh as Buffy looked a bit surprised.

"Girl, we need to talk." Buffy took Linda to a table and I presumed she was going to question her and break the news to her. I had everything I needed from Linda for now; Buffy can get what she can from her.

About fifteen minutes later, Trapper showed up.

"You must have broken a few speeding laws?"

"Traffic was light, and I knew where you were. Now where is this lady investigator?"

I pointed to Buffy and Trapper eye balled her. She was a looker, dark blonde hair, tall, well built, wearing tight jeans and a silk blouse. She was just perfect for Trapper. He grinned at me and said hi to Penny.

"Pull your tongue in, Will," Penny said. "And close your mouth."

"What's her name?"

"Buffy McCabe," I answered.

He looked to me and said, "Buffy?"

"Yep, and she's no bubble-head. So be careful. She's also a lot younger than you."

"Age means nothing to me, if she's smart enough I can get to like her."

"If she can get to like you." Penny put in.

"Hey, what's not to like, I'm good looking, smart, a private investigator and a good lover, what more can she want?"

"Someone who is not you," Penny said with a laugh.

"Yes and I love you too Penny."

"Either way, she'll have to decide. Ah, she's done with the waitress," I said. Buffy stood leaving Linda looking sad. I presumed Buffy gave her all the gory details that I had spared her from. Buffy came back to us.

"Buffy, this is Will Trapper, an old friend and partner in my firm. He's a retired cop from Michigan and working with me here now. He also is originally from Las Vegas, so if you need to know anything about the city, he can help."

I was sure Trapper was a bit put off by my references to him being an 'old friend' and 'retired', but he smiled and turned to her and said, "Good to meet you, I'm at your disposal."

"Will, I'm glad to meet you. Are you on any case right now?" she said with a smile.

"No, I happen to be free and open to suggestions."

"I could use someone to guide me around the city if you are interested?"

"I'd be more than happy to. When do you want to start?"

"We just did, now can you guide me to the dance floor?"

The band had started with a slow song, a belly rubber as I called it. They went to the dance floor and did their thing. I looked to Penny and she was smiling.

"Will is so smooth, but I don't think Buffy is so stupid to fall for his smoothness," I said. "She's going to use him."

"But he'll love it," Penny laughed. "What ever happened to Samantha?"

"They're taking some time off from each other. Trapper felt like she was getting too close."

"Will is going to be an old man with no one to love. He's never been married has he?"

"Nope, but he had a big love back here in Vegas years ago, she was killed in a traffic accident. I guess he never got over it."

"That's sad, I really hope he finds someone."

"Yep, but someone closer to his age, Buffy would probably kill him," I said with a big grin.

The band was now getting into a more lively country tune, something by Brooks and Dunn. Trapper and Buffy lasted on the dance floor for a couple more tunes, but Will was looking a little winded, he held up. They came back to us and sat.

Trapper leaned back and turned his head to me, "I guess I'm getting a bit old for all this."

"Will, you're only fifty-nine and in good health, dancing shouldn't kill you."

"I spend too much time fighting crime by the seat of my pants," he laughed.

Buffy must have good hearing, she said, "Will, we need to get you out doing some cardio and exercise. Tomorrow we start you on a regime of getting back into the shape I think you once were. Agreed?"

He looked back to her and had a surprised expression, "Okay, anything you say. I'm putty in your hands."

I leaned to Penny and said, "Smooth."

We hung in for about another two hours, boot-scootin the dance floor. I was surprised that Penny could do the line dance; she explained it was part of one of her shows a few years back. She had a country line-dance team on her show and they gave her a few lessons. Trapper and Buffy seemed to be enjoying each other, I had to admit it looked like a father and daughter out for a night. But he didn't care.

We were at a table now when Linda came rushing up and whispered in my ear, "Ricky's wife is here."

Chapter 7

I turned my attention to Buffy and said, "Do you know what Mary Lou looks like?"

"I've only heard about her, haven't had the pleasure to meet her yet, why?" she replied.

"Well, she's here. Shall we go greet her?"

Buffy looked surprised, not a good look for an investigator, we have to always be prepared for surprises and not show it. She had a lot to learn. "Where is she?" Buffy asked.

"I don't know yet, but Linda told me she was here, so I assume we ask Linda to point her out," I said as I stood and went to Linda waiting on a table. Buffy followed.

"Linda, where is Mary Lou?" I asked.

Linda pointed to a woman standing at the end of the bar in the corner. I turned to see a heavyset woman, about thirty-some, ratty hair and generally scary looking. I couldn't see what Ricky saw in her if he really was married to her. I didn't know what Jenny in Arizona looked like, I hoped better than Mary Lou.

Buffy followed me to the end of the bar and around it to the corner where Mary Lou was now sitting on a stool. "Excuse me, are you Mary Lou?" I said to start a conversation.

She gave me a dirty look and said, "Maybe, who's

asking?" she growled, just enough to cause shivers in my back.

I pulled my wallet with my investigator's license and the LVMPD auxiliary police badge that I had from back when I helped chase down the Bridezilla killer. Captain Weber had told Lynn to deputize me and she did, giving me the badge. No one ever asked for it back so I just figured it would be handy someday, or until I got caught.

I flashed both and said "I'm investigating the murder of Ricky Lawless, I understand that you are claiming to be his wife."

She gave me an evil-eye look and snarled, "I don't claim it, I am, or was, his wife. What's it to you?"

"As I said I'm investigating his murder, I'd like to talk about you and Ricky. How long were you married to him?"

"Are you a real cop, that badge said auxiliary."

Busted.

"I'm a private investigator and an auxiliary police officer, now I'm being nice here. I just need some answers, and I'd like to have a nice talk with you about it. Either here or I can have you taken in to Metro headquarters for questioning, your choice."

She mulled that over a bit, probably wondering how far my powers go with the badge. "Alright, we can talk. I was married to Ricky for about a year, since he started recording. He was on the road a lot, and I only saw him when he was close enough for me to drive from LA to where he was working. He was in Vegas and I come up to see him a couple times in the last three weeks."

Honky Tonk Murders

"You were here the night he died?"

"I wasn't in the bar, I was out exploring Vegas, I took in a couple shows. I missed the incident, and I didn't know about it until the next day."

"Witnesses say they saw you arguing with Ricky a couple nights before he was murdered, what was that about?"

She looked like she was chewing on something, I hoped gum and not chewing tobacco, she looked like she could. She took a drink from her glass then set it down. She looked to Buffy who was standing just behind me to my right.

"What's she, an auxiliary cop too?"

Buffy moved closer and said, "No, I'm an investigator for the company that insured Ricky's life. I'm here to investigate his death for payment of the policy."

"Well, I should be a rich woman, shouldn't I?"

Now I spoke, "Not really, Ricky's real wife, the one in Arizona may have something to say about that. She's listed as his beneficiary."

Now Mary Lou showed a crack in her composure, "What wife in Arizona?"

"The woman he's been married to for the last sixteen years and has a fifteen year old daughter with; that wife in Arizona. You didn't know?"

"Buster, if I knew I would have killed him myself, which I didn't. The rat bastard married me when we met in LA while he was performing at a dive there. I took a shine to him and let him stay at my house near Echo Park. We got married in a fever, as the song goes. He stayed with me until he had to tour. I paid for most of his expenses and tour equipment; I had quite a bit of money from a former husband in a divorce settlement. Son of a bitch, he used me." She took a good swallow of her drink.

"Want to know what we were arguing about? Money. He was spending what I gave him to get his records made, but in the wrong places. I was complaining that I wasn't seeing any return on my investment from his record sales. He bellyached that his company was hanging on to his royalties; he would pay me back when he got them. But he was spending my money like he was some rich bastard and I called him on it."

"Did you know of anyone who may have wanted to kill him?" Buffy asked.

"Lady, I couldn't tell you about any of his friends, let alone enemies. He didn't share much with me. I often wondered why I even married him. But I knew it was for my money." She slurped up the rest of her drink and slammed the glass down calling to the cowgirl behind the bar for another and continued, "I just figured he be a big country star someday, he was good, that's what attracted me to him.

"Did you know any of the people at his record company?" I asked.

"Just two, Jeb Hawley and Sam Casper, they were his reps at the Circle Four Records. They were in a club in LA when he came back to perform in town and they showed up while I was there. They seemed to be snake oil salesmen to me, but I didn't care as long as they could make him a star. I did hear them talking about insurance against his not fulfilling the contract. They had him sign some papers for it too. Ricky bragged to me later that he was worth about ten million dollars in record sales even if he couldn't perform, just on his record sales. Want to investigate killers, I'd look to them." Her second drink arrived and she belted it down.

"If you don't need me, I think I'll go buy a fifth of whiskey and retire to my motel room."

I asked where she was staying and she told me, then she went off and out the front door.

"I'll call my friend in Vegas homicide to go check her out." I turned to see Trapper standing behind us, smiling. "You probably loved that didn't you?" I asked him.

"That was some great interrogation techniques. I learn so much from you." He said with a grin.

I turned to Buffy and said, "Get him out of my sight." I went back to Penny who was relaxing in her chair with about five people sitting with her. Fans I hoped. Penny smiled up to me as I stood next to her.

"I think we are done here, shall we go home to see if Willy has destroyed the house?"

She gave me a frown and stood, thanking her fans and we went out the front door to the van. I sat in the seat as I pulled my cell phone and called Lynn. I explained what had happened in the bar and gave her the name of the motel where Mary Lou was staying. She thanked me and said she would look into it. I hung up and put the phone back in my pocket. I turned to Penny and blew her a kiss.

"You didn't marry me for my money, did you?" Penny asked after listening to my detailed report to Lynn.

"I sure did, if you remember I was broke and living with my parents. So what did you expect?"

She reached over and slapped my arm and said, "Let's go home, I'm beat."

I drove out and into our driveway letting Penny out at the front door. The security lights came on so Penny could see if there was anyone lurking by the front door, there wasn't. I parked the van on the side and could see Angelo in the guesthouse, his front windows weren't covered. That would bother me in the dark of the night.

I locked up the van, went in the side door directly to the kitchen and was expecting a mess. I was surprised to see Willy sitting quietly in the middle of the room, tail wagging furiously. Penny was standing at the kitchen door from the front smiling.

"He didn't even poop on the floor. Take him out before he explodes." Penny said and went off from the room.

I picked up Willy and took him out the back door to the side where he relieved himself. I smiled and said, "You are being good for some reason? Maybe you want us to take you with us more often?"

"Who you talking to Mr. R.?" came a gruff voice from the gate in the fence, it was Angelo. He startled me.

"Hey Angelo, I was talking to Willy, how's things going with you?" I said recovering from my surprise.

"Good, Buck has me guarding some country

singer from Nashville. I start tomorrow morning, when she comes into McCarron Airport. I'm not much for country music but it's still a job I will do."

"And I know you will do it well, my friend."

*

Chapter 8

Willy had finished his business and I picked it up with the plastic bag I brought out with me. Angelo was standing nearby and laughed as Willy bounced around his feet.

"Dis dog is so cute, I may be wanting to get one of my own, but I'm kinda busy most da time." Angelo said slipping back into his mob talk. He had been improving his speech, but occasionally it was nice to hear the vernacular from his former life.

"Well you can babysit Willy anytime you have nothing to do. It gets a little hard to take him out on a case, I'm afraid he might get hurt."

"No problem, be glad ta watch him."

"Thanks, my friend. Well, I need to go get some sleep. I'm investigating the murder of a country singer, so we may run into each other over the weekend at the country music awards show. You sleep well yourself, those country female singers can be a handful, just don't take any guff."

"I'll keep a tight fist on them, thanks, sleep good."

He went back to his little house and I took Willy back inside to call it a night.

I was lying in bed, Penny was already asleep, she was a fast sleeper. Me, I just couldn't nod off as fast, I thought too much in the quiet of the night. I was going over the events of the day and came up with a few observations that I should have checked earlier. First, how did Ricky's insurance company know so soon after he died, and how did Buffy get there the day after it happened? Who called them and why? I also thought about talking to the band that performed with Ricky that night; I should have talked to them earlier. I guess I'm getting old and forgetful to not come up with such basic questions. But I had to admit there were a lot of distractions tonight, hard to concentrate on the details when the bigger picture was glaring in my face.

I must have finally dozed off, because Penny was shaking me in bed telling me to get up. She went off to the kitchen, I presumed, because I could hear pans being used. Angelo was making one of his famous breakfasts for us. I got up slowly, letting my body and bones creak into place. I stood slowly stretching my body into an upright position, it hurt briefly. Damn, I hated getting old.

I showered first before going to breakfast, then ambled out to the snack bar where I found a plate of pancakes waiting for me.

"Good morning Mr. R., I hope ya gotta good night's sleep," Angelo said as he put the syrup in front of me.

"Yes I did Angelo, slept through the night. I didn't even get up to use the bathroom, which means I slept soundly. What time do you have to go pick-up your client?"

"Da lady is coming in around noon, so I gots some time left."

Penny was just finishing her pancakes and asked me, "So where are we investigating today?"

I swallowed the food in my mouth and said, "I need to call Jenny in Arizona to ask a few questions first that came to me last night. Then I'll figure out where to go from there."

Angelo had finished putting the pots and pans away and said he was going to get ready for his job. He went off leaving Penny, Willy and I still finishing our breakfast.

"You don't think we're taking advantage of Angelo with these breakfasts, do you?"

"Penny dear, he is living in our guesthouse rent free; I don't think he minds the payback."

"I guess so, it's nice having him nearby, for company and protection. If I had to have any person protecting us, it would be Angelo."

"Hey, I'm good at protecting too, you know."

"Yes dear, but you're getting slow at moving, we'd be tied up and the house robbed before you'd have your gun out."

"Yeah, well, you'd have your gun out before crooks would even get a chance to tie us up."

"Count on it Sweetie," she said with her evil little smile and went off to get dressed.

I looked down to Willy and said, "Women, it'd be

a far better world without them. Beer and TV every night, not having to clean up after ourselves and there'd be no murders committed in the name of love. Nasty thing love, makes people do stupid things. Don't you agree?"

Willy was doing his shaking thing and yipped to me. I smiled and threw the pup a piece of pancake.

About an hour later, I was fully dressed and in my home office at my desk. Penny was sitting in the chair facing me as I picked up the phone to call Jenny. I didn't know how to tell her that Ricky was not a faithful husband, even to the point of marrying another woman.

"Ricky was a bastard," Penny said, surprising me with her outburst. I paused in my dialing and asked why.

"He was married to my cousin for sixteen years and had a daughter, but he married this woman from LA just for her money, so he's a bastard," she said with a bit of disgust.

"You won't get an argument from me. I guess that makes it easier to tell her, but I don't want to hurt her."

"Let me break it to her, then you can ask your questions."

I liked that idea, Penny was better at talking to people about unpleasant things. I finished dialing and put the thing on speakerphone, so we could both listen.

The phone on the other end rang a number of times before Jenny answered. She said hello and Penny moved closer to the phone base.

"Jenny, this is your cousin Penny. Do you have some time to talk?"

"Sure, Kelly is still sleeping now," she replied. I presumed Kelly was the daughter, I hadn't asked before. She continued, "Did you find out anything about Ricky?"

"Well, we found out a number of things. First I have to ask something and I hope you'll be honest with me, how was your marriage to Ricky going?"

There was a long awkward pause from the phone; we waited. Finally, Jenny said, "We were having problems, him being gone way too long at a time, and with Kelly being sick he was hardly there for her. I was doubting our relationship, he was distant when he was home, like he wanted to be on the road. I know he loved the singing and the performing, but it hurt me to have him not want us in that life." She took a breath and paused again.

"Take your time, Jen. I'll wait," Penny said softly.

"Penny, you have a good marriage from what I hear, but my marriage hasn't been. I was almost on the verge of divorcing him, but then his records started to take off, I figured he'd at least pay the hospital bills for Kelly. That was the only reason I put up with his crap."

She was sounding a bit bitter now, making it easier for Penny to announce the final blow.

"Jen, I have something to tell you, it's not easy for me to say to you, so I'll just tell you. Ricky had married another woman out in Los Angeles about a year ago. It turns out he just married her for the money she gave him." Penny paused for a reaction.

"I'm not surprised, I could tell he was up to something. I just didn't think he'd do something so stupid as to marry another woman. Thanks for telling me."

That was easy, now I need to ask a few questions. "Jenny this is Jim, can I ask you a few questions?"

"Sure, go ahead, this is all a big mess anyways, I hope you can straighten it out."

"How did you find out Ricky was dead?"

"I got a call from one of the guys who played in his band, Buster Jones. He was a good friend to Ricky and me, so he called to tell me."

"Did you call his insurance company right away?"

"No, I still haven't talk to anyone there until I heard from you."

"Well, could Buster have called them?"

"I don't know why he would, I don't even know if Ricky told any of his band who he was insured through."

"Does this band travel with him?"

"Just Buster and another man named Geech Goodwin, his drummer. Buster played bass and Ricky was lead guitar. They would hire a steel guitar player while in towns that had good musicians to fill out the sound. Just Buster and Geech traveled with him."

Buster and Geech, sounds like a country team I thought. "There is an investigator from the insurance company in town to investigate the cause of death, so if we find Ricky hadn't committed suicide, there should be a double payout on his policy. Did you know how much he was insured for?"

"No, he never talked about that, he said it creeped him out to talk about death."

"Okay are you sitting?"

She paused, "Yes I am."

"Ricky's basic policy was a death payment of three million dollars, with double indemnity it will be six million."

We heard what sounded like the phone dropping and then could hear some coughing sounds. The phone was picked up again and Jenny said loudly, "Six million dollars! Oh… my… God, how can that be?"

"It's what he felt he was worth, now you are a wealthy woman."

*

Chapter 9

We calmed Jenny down enough to explain to her that she should call the insurance company to arrange for a payout, after Buffy finished her investigating that is. We could tell Jenny was crying, probably thinking about how she was going to be able to take full care of her daughter now.

"I'm still not finished checking a few things here, but I'll let you know what is going on. Now we have to discuss getting Ricky's body back to you. Have you contacted the funeral home?" I asked.

"Yes, I call yesterday; they said they'd take care of burial after he is brought out. Are you still going to do that?"

"Yes, we can. Is Ricky's recording label in LA?" I asked.

"No, they have a studio in Phoenix. Ricky recorded all his songs there. His agent is there also."

"Have you talked to them at all?"

"No, and as I said before they haven't even called to express their regrets. I never liked them anyways."

"Okay, I have to find out the final outcome of his body then we'll get him back to you."

"Jim, I was thinking about it, I think I want him cremated and then brought back. Right now, with what you told me, I really don't want to see him laid out. Kelly's health is too bad to even leave the hospital to see him anyways. I want her to just remember her father when he was alive. Can you see about cremation out there?"

That would make things so much easier to take him home. "I'll call a person who I know at a mortuary here and arrange it. I'll let you know how it works out."

"Thank you Jim and Penny, I appreciate your help." She sounded like she was choking up again.

"Go rest now and we'll take care of everything for you," Penny said and we hung up.

I sat back thinking how this woman must be a wreck now with everything going on. I hoped six million dollars would help her. Penny was sitting back also and smiled at me. "You're going to call Hannigan Mortuary aren't you?"

Honky Tonk Murders

She knew I would, Hannigan was the man who started my case on the missing body from his mortuary that led to tracking down a dirty bomb and a hired assassin bent on killing the President while he was visiting Vegas. Fun times, I mused.

"Yes, I'll have him take care of the details. Now I have to see what Lynn may have come up with talking to Mary Lou. Care to go for a ride?"

"Sure and I think we need to take Willy out for a ride too."

"Works for me, but you get to carry his bag," I said as I stood and came around the desk. We went out to the kitchen and Willy was sitting in the middle of the room, next to his travel bag. I was startled.

"How did he get that down from the counter?" I asked.

"He's our baby, he's resourceful." Nothing much seemed to faze Penny; she took most unexplained things in stride.

I picked up the bag and Willy was bouncing. I picked him up and put him in the opening and handed the bag to Penny. We went out the front door after I set the time delay on the driveway alarm.

We drove out to the LV Metro police precinct where we found Lynn sitting in her office typing on the computer. She looked to us and grinned.

"Why did I have a strange feeling you two would be here soon?" she said.

"We radiate warmth where ever we go, what do you have on Mary Lou?"

"Nothing, she flew the coop last night by the time I got there. I got a BOLO out for her and called the

LA police to watch for her. She just put herself up high on my list of suspects for murder."

"I probably should have called you from the bar when we knew she was there," I said sheepishly.

"That would have been nice, but I realize you are getting senile. So I'll forgive you this time. Did you get anything from the insurance dick?"

"Not much, she was about as clueless as we were. I know Trapper may have some more information from her. They hung in at the bar after Penny and I left."

"You left her with Trapper, was that wise?"

"I think he'll survive. She seems to be pretty aggressive. I'll find out when I see him later. So your case on Ricky hasn't much more than I got?"

"Nope, we talked to everyone who was there that night and no one saw him take any drinks other than the water glass on the stage. CSI found the glass and they said it was good old tap water, no sign of poison. The only answer is that someone switched the glass after he keeled over. There was such confusion it could have been easy for someone to grab the glass and switch it out."

"Are you done with Ricky's body yet, I have directions to have the body cremated before taking it back to Arizona."

"Cremated, eh?' I was always suspicious of cremations, the body is then long gone for further examinations. Was this the wife's idea?"

"Yes, but I think she had good reasons for it. Besides you got all the samples you need from such an open and shut case of the cause of the murder."

"Yeah, we do know he was poisoned by ingestion, that's pretty much determined, but I'm always suspicious of cremation. Who you going to have do it?"

"Hannigan Mortuary, I'm sure you remember them."

"No, not really, your memory is slipping if you don't remember, I was in LA testifying on a trial, Deacon helped on most of that case."

"Right, how is Deacon doing, by the way?"

"I passed him in the hallway, we snuck a kiss and he said he was going out to bust a few hookers. I hope he doesn't catch anything."

"Is your relationship doing better now?" Penny asked.

"Oh, yes. We are so glad to see each other now when we get home, makes for more pleasant evenings."

Penny laughed and said, "I can imagine what your pleasant evenings entailed."

"Deacon chasing after hookers stirs his libido too," she said with a laugh.

Captain Weber popped in the door and said, "Richards, and Mrs. Richards, good to see you, I hear you are investigating our country singer's death also?"

"Yes, the singer's wife is Penny's cousin, she asked us to look into it. Are you a big fan of country?"

"If you consider Elvis to be country I am. But I admire the sound of a good country tune, so carry on," he said and flew out the door.

"I've said it before and again, that is one strange man," I said again.

"So what are you going to do now?" Lynn asked.

"Heading to the mortuary and see Hannigan, then later we might go back to the bar and talk to a couple friends of Ricky's. Care to join us and bring Deacon?"

"We just might do that, we haven't been out in a while and this way I kill two birds with one line dance."

"Great, I'll call when we are ready to go." I turned to Penny still holding a very quiet Willy in his bag and said, "Shall we go to the death house?"

"Not when you put it like that, fool."

"Okay let's go visit Mr. Hannigan."

"Better, see you later Lynn," she said and we went out.

I remembered where the mortuary was since Penny and I first went there, back when I called Penny my assistant and she wasn't happy about it. We parked and went in to find the same receptionist as before and she smiled when we entered.

"Mr. and Mrs. Richards, good to see you again, are you here on a case?"

"Sort of but this doesn't involve your business. We have a body that needs cremating; you do that here don't you?"

"Oh yes, we are licensed to cremate bodies, and we have the best technology to prevent the foul smoke from our crematorium," she said with a sense of pride.

"Is Mr. Hannigan in?" I asked.

"I'll get him," she said as she picked up her phone and made the call.

About five minutes later Thomas Hannigan came through the door and welcomed us. We went to his office and he had us sit.

"What can I do for you today?" he asked.

"We have a body that needs cremating," I said

"Someone you killed?" he said with a grin.

"No, but I 'm investigating his death. He's a cousin of Penny's and we are going to take him back home to Phoenix, after you cremate him."

"Where is he now?"

"Clark County Morgue, he'll be released soon, I'll let you know. Can you have someone pick him up?"

"I sure can," he said as he pushed a pad of paper and pencil towards me. "Just put his name down and I'll arrange the rest. What type of container do you want him in?"

"Coffee can would be fine," I joked, Penny whacked my arm and I winced. "Sorry, what do you have?"

He pulled out a booklet and showed us the selection. I moved it to Penny and told her to pick one. She thumbed through it like it was a Sears' catalogue and then pointed to one that looked nice.

I saw the price and said, "Remember dear, you said he was a bastard."

She gave me a stare that told me to shut up, and said, "He left my cousin six million dollars, we can at least inter his remains with dignity."

She showed Hannigan the one she liked and said to go with it. He smiled and said he had a few of them on hand, so it was no problem.

"How long after you pick him up will he be ready for transport to Phoenix?" I asked.

"Well, you'll have to sign a few papers at the morgue to release the body and for a transfer permit; it would be the next day after we take him in. I can call you when it's done. I still have your business card from our adventure with the missing body, thank you so much for your help on that."

I almost thought about asking for a discount on the urn for helping him, but I knew Penny would just whack me again, so I kept quiet about that and said, "No problem, that was a definite adventure." We finished and left the building.

*

Chapter 10

I sat for a moment in the van until Penny finally asked what I was doing. "I'm organizing my thoughts."

"That shouldn't take this long," she said with a sigh.

"Sorry, but I like to have a plan before I just stumbled blindly into the fray."

"Fray? Are you trying to be poetic now?"

"I'm trying to figure out my attack on this. Do you have a better idea?"

She sighed again, "Why don't you go to the morgue and see what Joe Lang has for you?"

"Just what I was thinking," I said with a sly glance to her.

I drove over to the morgue and we went in, leaving Willy in the van. The morgue was no place for a dog, with all the doggy maladies that could be caught. A morgue is not the most sanitary place. At least that was our excuse for not bringing him.

Joe Lang grinned when he saw Penny; I got a stare. "What? You aren't happy to see me too?" I said.

"Don't push it, you make me work," he said finally smiling.

"Is Ricky's body ready for transfer?"

"Yes he is. If you'll follow me we can get the paperwork finished for you to take him. You got a mortuary to pick him up, oh wait, you got Hannigan to take him didn't you?"

"Only mortician I know personally. I'll call him and say we did the paperwork."

"How are you transporting the body to Phoenix?"

"He's going in a seven inch square urn."

"You're having him cremated?"

"That's the widow's wishes and it's easier to haul him back home."

"I don't remember any country songs about being cremated?"

"I thought they always had a way of sending a cheating husband to hell."

Joe laughed and gave me the papers to sign. We finished up and were back to the van. Willy was sitting in my driver's seat and wouldn't move. "You aren't old enough to drive, now get to the floor."

He huffed and jumped down. I slid in and Penny was already buckled in. "I think he understands you, Sweetie."

"Too bad his mother doesn't."

"I'm not his mother, I'm more of a younger sister."

"Dream on," I said as I started the van and drove out. We went by the office, I saw Trapper's Jeep in the parking lot next to a Subaru. I presumed it was Buffy's.

"What's Will doing here on a Saturday?" Penny asked.

"I'd hate to imagine. I think the Subaru probably belongs to Buffy."

"And they are here? What's wrong with Will's apartment?"

"Well, lets go find out," I said with a smirk.

We came in the back door quietly and could hear nothing. We went up to Trapper's door and I peeked around the doorframe. They weren't in there. I signaled to Penny to follow and went up front. We found them sitting on the couch in the lobby watching TV. I had to laugh which made Trapper jump.

"What are you two doing?" I asked.

"Just watching the Great American Country station about the CMA awards tomorrow night. Why are you two here?"

"Just slumming. How was your night?" I said quietly as Penny went to sit with Buffy.

"Well, I'm not in love but I enjoyed her company," he said with a grin.

"You are a letch, you know that."

"Yes, and proud of it." We went to the couch and sat. Trapper squeezed in between Penny and Buffy. Penny grinned and moved over next to me.

"So Buffy what's your report going to say?" I asked.

"I don't see anything out of the ordinary, he was poisoned by a killer, so the policy's double indemnity is standing. We just need to find out who was the killer before we can release the funds."

I knew that was coming, they had to be sure the beneficiary didn't murder the policy holder, or arrange it. Now I had to work harder to find the killer so Jenny could get her money. Damn, I hated pressure.

"Okay, are you going to be hanging around for the finale?"

"Of course, I have to prove my worth to the company. This may be my last job if I don't bring home something."

"Are they threatening you?" Penny asked.

"Not really, but I probably will end up in actuary filing cases if I don't come back with the goods."

I could feel both Penny and Trapper looking at me after she said that. "Okay, stick close and we'll help you beat the system," I said.

"Thank you, I was hoping you would help."

"I have a question, how did your company find out so quickly that Ricky was dead?"

"They got a phone call from an anonymous person that he had been murdered. Since the policy involved so much money, they jumped quickly to cover their butts. I was sent out since I was the only agent who wasn't already on a case. I drove out the next day and here I am."

A mysterious caller? I thought about Buster again, he was probably the only person who would have called, but what did he hope to gain? Well, I'd have to ask later when we talked to the band.

"So now what do we do? Mary Lou has flown the coup, and we have no other suspects. I need to talk to Ricky's band members to see what they have to offer. In a day or two, I'll be taking the body back to Phoenix and I'm going to inquire at his recording company and his agent as to their interest in his death." I leaned forward and asked Buffy, "If you'd care to tag along. It's okay by me."

"Thanks, if you think it will help, I'm for it." She looked to Trapper and he smiled and said, "I guess I could escort you out to Arizona if you'd like."

She said quietly but we could hear, "I like."

There was nothing much more to do until the bar had the band in to play later tonight, so I invited everyone to our home for a barbecue. They all agreed and we drove out to the house. I was wondering how Angelo was doing with his country client and would have to give him a call later.

I fired up the incinerator as we call the B-B-Q grill and cooked the steaks we had for special occasions. Penny and Buffy worked on some side dish and then we had a picnic in the back. Life was good.

Honky Tonk Murders

Penny talked Buffy into swimming in the pool; I swear she was going to get everyone into it. Trapper and I just sat admiring the women swimming about. Around six, I said we should get ready to go talk to the band. The women got dressed and I took Penny in the van, Trapper took Buffy in his Jeep to the bar once again.

We entered the bar and I saw Linda working the tables. She smiled when she saw us and came over to seat us. She took our drink orders but before she left she said, "The police were here a little while ago asking about Mary Lou. She's missing."

"Yes we know, you don't know where she may be?" I asked.

"Like I told that lady detective, I don't. Does this mean she murdered Ricky?"

"No, but she is a suspect now."

"Okay, I'll get your drinks," she said and went off.

I was watching the band getting their equipment set up and decided to wait a bit before questioning them. I had called Lynn about meeting us here for some dancing and relaxing, maybe they needed it. About twenty minutes later Lynn and Deacon came in and sat with us.

"I hear you were in here earlier questioning Linda about Mary Lou?" I asked.

"Yes, that was a lot of nothing, too. Still no word about her, she's still odds on for the crime. She probably found out Ricky was married and he was taking her for her money, so easy to see she did it."

I looked to Buffy, "There, your case is solved."

She asked Lynn, "Can I get that in writing?"

"No, not until we find her and beat her into confessing, then you'll get your written statement. By the way who are you?"

"I'm sorry Lynn this is Buffy McCabe, insurance investigator for Western Life. She's making sure Ricky wasn't murdered by his wife, the real one."

"Nice to meet you Buffy, this is my partner Deacon DeAngelo. I hope you're not trying to learn investigation techniques from Jim."

"Hey, who is it that you call on when you can't get a handle on your cases. Me, that's who."

"Don't flatter yourself. Now who is this person in the band who called your cousin?"

"His name is Buster Jones. He plays bass guitar." I looked over and the only man with a bass was just putting his instrument on the stand, picked up a glass and went to the bar. He ran some water into the glass from the bar spritzer and took a drink. I stood and went to him.

"Buster?"

"Yep, what can I do for you?"

"My wife is Ricky's wife's cousin. Can I talk to you?"

"Jenny's cousin? Sure I can talk."

"Follow me," I said and went back to my table. He followed.

I pulled up a chair for Buster to sit next to me and he sat.

"Buster this is my wife, Penny, she's Jenny's cousin. This woman is homicide Lieutenant Lynn Carter from the Las Vegas Metro Police and she is investigating the murder of Ricky. I was asked by Jenny to look into his death, so if you could answer a few questions about the night Ricky died, it would be helpful."

He sat looking a little surprised, then said, "I don't know much about that night, I just saw him fall off the stage and then they said he was dead. That's all I know."

"Well, you called Jenny the next day to tell her and I believe you called Ricky's insurance company to tell them. How am I doing?"

He sat staring at the floor and then quietly said, "Yes, I did."

*

Chapter 11

"I can see calling Jenny, but why did you call the insurance company?"

"I knew Jenny was having money problems with Kelly in the hospital and Ricky wasn't sending much money to her, so I figured seeing as Ricky was dead, rest his soul, she could use the cash. Ricky once tried to get me to sign up for insurance through his insurance man, but I didn't. That's how I knew what company it was."

Lynn spoke up now, "Very noble of you, Jenny will benefit now. Of course, this makes you look like a suspect too, trying to help Jenny. Maybe you didn't like Ricky that much?"

"Hey lady, I loved Ricky like a brother, I'd never do anything to hurt him. Okay, I took advantage of a bad situation, but Jenny needed the help. Unless you're arresting me for something, I need to get ready for my set." He stood and went back to the stage.

"I think I hit a nerve," Lynn said. "I need some more information from him. I'll let him coast for now, but tomorrow I'm hauling him in for more questioning."

"You're just such a softy aren't you?" I said. I turned to Buffy and said, "Now you know who placed the call, you can put that in your report."

"Well, it's something," she said with a half smile.

I looked over to the bar and saw the drummer, Geech, getting a glass of something from the bar's drink hose. I excused myself and went to him.

"Excuse me, you're Geech?"

"So I've been told, whatcha want?" He had a slight southern drawl not as bad as what I had heard from my book tour through the south.

"I'm a cousin to Jenny, wife of Ricky Lawless, I'm also a private investigator hired by Jenny to find out what happened to her husband. Got a minute to talk?"

"The police have already talked to me, but if you think it will do any good, sure." He followed my lead to the table and I had him sit in the chair that Buster had sat in moments ago.

He looked to Lynn and smiled, "You're that lady cop I talked to the other day."

Lynn smiled back and said she was. "We just

need to follow up on a few more details, if you don't mind?"

"I don't mind at all, if it helps catch the bastard who killed Ricky."

I spoke now, "Tell me, what happened that night Ricky died?"

He turned his body towards me in the chair with his back now to Lynn; I saw that as an expression that he may not like women in authority, or cops, but I'm no psychiatrist.

"Well, we got up on stage to perform and Ricky was into the fourth song, a great number he wrote hisself, and then he just leaned forward and fell off the stage. I knew he didn't drink the hard stuff to be drunk, so something was wrong. I got up from behind my drum set and went around to him. I checked him but he was dead. Buster yelled to the waitress to call someone, we didn't know who to alert, the cops or an ambulance, seeing as he was already dead. I guess the waitress called 911 and they sent both the cops and the medical people. I just stood back and watched."

"The police know that he was poisoned, did you see him drink anything before he started to perform?"

"Just his water he always had on the stool behind him, it was the only thing I saw him drink that night."

"What happened to the glass of water after Ricky died?"

"Couldn't say, I wasn't watching for it. The police told us not to touch anything, so we didn't. Then all those crime scene investigators came in and were checking everything on the stage. I guess they may have taken it."

"Did Ricky have any enemies?"

"Hell, Ricky was loved by everyone. I can't name a single person who would want to harm the man. He was kind, friendly and would do anything for a friend."

"What do you know about this wife named Mary Lou?"

He got a little stiff on that question; he looked down to the floor and then said, "I thought it was the only thing Ricky did that wasn't right. He took on that woman as a wife when he was already married to Jenny. Wasn't right, but he explained it was just for the money, to help us get established in the recording business. I hoped Jenny would never find out, it wasn't right."

Lynn said from behind him, "Did that make you mad?"

He didn't turn, just brought his head up and said to me, "I wasn't happy about it, it wasn't legal, or right, but he did it anyways. The money did help us get new equipment and get the records made, so I just bit my tongue and went along with it. I figured God would punish him for it, not with death, but he'd regret it in the afterlife."

"You believe in the afterlife?" I asked him.

"Sure, don't you?" he replied.

"I'll form an opinion if I ever get there. Do you think Mary Lou may have had something to do with his death?"

"Could be, she was in town on that day and was arguing with him just before we were to perform. She left before we got on stage, I don't know where she went, but she wasn't here. I haven't seen her since."

"Who did you get to replace Ricky?"

"We had a kid who followed us and he did some roadie work too. He has a good voice and knew all the songs, so we gave him a shot and he did well. He's singing tonight with us. I have to go get ready for the first set so if you don't have anything more, I need to go."

"No, I'm fine for now, but I may have a few more questions later, if you don't mind?"

"Nope, just catch the bastard who did it, I'll be glad to help string him or her up." He stood and went to the stage as we sat watching him go.

"We got a few more suspects now, wouldn't you say?" Lynn spoke first.

"The waitress could be a killer too; Ricky said he was going to marry her after he divorced his LA wife. I'm not believing that Ricky was all as nice as people make him out to be. And there's the kid singer who took over for Ricky, he may have done it for the job. We may find a lot more skeletons in his closet before we finish." I took a long swig of my beer and turned to Penny. "Still with us?"

"How can I ignore such an intriguing plot? All the elements of a great country song." She leaned over and kissed my nose.

I looked to Buffy and said, "So what do your investigating skills tell you?"

She smiled and said, "Well, you got Mary Lou who was angry with Ricky for spending her money foolishly, she may have even found out about Jenny. Then you got Buster who didn't like the treatment

Jenny was getting back in Arizona. Geech wasn't happy with the arrangement Ricky had with his sinful lifestyle. Now you got a waitress who may have been mad enough at the promise of marriage to a bigamist that she could have poisoned his drink and some kid who may have wanted to take Ricky's place. So I have no idea who to say did it."

"Welcome to our world," Trapper said. "Don't forget the wounded wife back in Arizona, she may have found out about Ricky's lifestyle and hired someone to do him in."

"Hey, that's my cousin you're talking about," Penny said.

"Just saying," Trapper defended.

"Besides, she didn't have any money to hire a killer," Penny added.

"Six million dollars is enough to hire any killer," I said.

"Now don't you start too," Penny said as she whacked my arm.

"Hey, you didn't hit Trapper when he brought it up."

"I'm not married to him, so I can hit you," she said with her evil little smile.

The band started playing and the kid got up and sang well. I had never heard Ricky so I couldn't compare. I figured that Lynn hadn't spoke to the kid, so we'd catch him on the break. We just sat for now enjoying the music. I wasn't a big fan of country but many of the songs were crossover nowadays and could be enjoyed by everyone. The music of Shania Twain started the big jump to pop music by a country singer that paved the way for more groups to embrace both sides of the music stream.

About forty minutes later the band finished and I went to the kid and asked him if he could join us. He looked a little skeptical, but Geech came up and told him that he should talk to us. The kid followed me to the table and I offered him a chair. I was getting tired of thinking of him as the kid, so I asked his name.

"Jericho Lane, but you can call me Jerry. What do you want to talk to me about?" he said with a wary smile.

I introduced everyone to him, leaving Lynn and Deacon last as I told him that they were police, and we were investigating the death of Ricky Lawless.

"I don't know anything about Ricky's death, but I think the wife did it," he said quickly.

A little too quickly I thought.

*

Chapter 12

"So you think the wife did it, why?" Lynn asked.

"She was a royal bitch, she threatened him a few times too. I was setting up the band's equipment one night in the last club we worked at a few months ago; she came by and started to scream at him for the amount of money he was spending on his lifestyle. Ricky defended himself saying he had to keep up a front for his image. You have to look good to do good. She was mean to him and I think she was mean enough to do the murder."

"Did you see her here the night Ricky died?" I asked.

"Sure, she pulled the same shit she always did, screaming and putting him down. She wasn't very supportive of his music. She thought it was a joke and was saying she wanted her money back or else."

"Or else what?" Lynn asked.

"She didn't say, she just stormed off and that was the last I saw of her, the night Ricky died."

"So if Ricky was poisoned, how could Mary Lou have poisoned him if she wasn't here?" I said to both Jerry and Lynn.

They thought about it for a moment, Jerry finally said, "I guess I could be wrong about her. She really didn't have the time to spike his drink." He went silent, thinking about that.

"Okay, so we may rule out Mary Lou as the killer," Lynn said.

"Doesn't say she didn't arrange it," Deacon said.

"Yeah, she had money to hire someone, maybe," I replied.

There came a voice over the band's speakers, it was Buster calling for Jerry to report to the stage. He stood and I thanked him for talking, than he went off.

"I think he did it," Deacon said.

"Why?" Lynn replied to his rather quick judgement.

"I just feel it, big rising star and the young newbie. He wanted the lime light and bumped off Ricky to get it," Deacon retorted.

"That may be, but this is not the band rising, it was Ricky and his voice, talent and he alone can't be replaced by a new person without that person rising up like Ricky did. Ricky's songs were his own so a new singer may sing the songs but may not be as popular." I said.

"I just think he still did it."

"Time will tell dear," Lynn said to him.

"I'm going for Mary Lou," Penny said.

"I thought we ruled her out, Jerry said she wasn't even here," I said.

"She had money, she could have hired someone poison him."

"Okay babe, that is possible." I kissed Penny on her cheek and she smiled. I looked around to everyone, "We all have our favorite killer now, shall we start a betting pool?"

"You're disgusting, a man was murdered and you want to bet on who was the killer? I'm in for twenty on Buster, he seems the type." Lynn grinned and sat back.

I looked to Penny, "Are you in?"

"Sure, twenty on Mary Lou," she replied.

"Who shall we have hold the money?" I asked.

Trapper said, "I think Buffy should, she's honest enough not to run off with the funds."

Buffy turned to Trapper, "Are you're really sure about that. I could use the extra cash."

The band started up loud, drowning out the rest of our conversation, which wasn't much. I sat back taking in Jerry's vocals and thinking he could go far with a bit more experience. He didn't work the audience very well, but he had potential. They finished the first number and then did a tribute to Ricky and his songs. People were up on the dance floor, doing the two-step and boot scooting to the music.

I noticed that Jerry was nervously watching us, probably hoping we would leave. Lynn and Deacon got up and did a couple turns on the dance floor. Trapper and I kidded about being too old to try to boot scoot, mostly because we'd look stupid trying it.

The band finished the set and everyone took their seats. We were making light conversation about country-dances when Lynn's cell phone played the theme from the old TV show 'Dragnet', one that she put it on her phone to let her know that murder was afoot. She answered and listened for a moment then hung up.

"Well, I guess Penny lost her bet, Mary Lou's body was just found in a dumpster off Maryland and Rochelle. Jim, isn't that the area you used to live in?"

"Yes, it is. How was she killed?" I replied.

"Throat cut, wide and deep. Body had to be dumped there, no amounts of blood around in the trash or by the dumpster." She looked to Deacon, "Well, you're in vice now, so I don't have to take you, but you can come just to give me moral support."

"Can we all come to give you moral support?" Trapper asked.

"Only if you stay out of my way. Shall we go?" Lynn stood and headed towards the back door followed by Deacon. The rest of us gathered our things and ran after her, she was in a hurry.

Honky Tonk Murders

As Lynn had said, I lived in an apartment complex around Maryland and Rochelle Street years back. It was a large place, just one of a dozen apartment complexes in that area, mostly occupied by Mexicans and low income Americans. I was one of the low income Americans who lived there back when I worked for Nick North's show at the Flamingo Hotel.

I drove Penny out in the van followed by Trapper and Buffy. Lynn was long gone, but I figured where she'd be by all the police black and whites infesting the place. We arrived and found the black and whites along with the coroner's van, with ME Joe Lang presiding over the body.

I parked the van on the street; Penny got out and followed me to the scene with Trapper and Buffy behind us. There was now a yellow tape border protecting the area, but the cop watching the barrier recognized us and let us pass. We stood just away from where the dumpster was and Mary Lou's body was now on the ground in front. Deacon saw us and came over.

"A resident of the building came out to dump her trash and discovered the body. She called 911 and waited here." He pointed to a short, wide Mexican woman talking to Lynn. "Joe's prelim estimate says that Mary Lou had to have been murdered sometime last night, over twenty four hours ago and just after we put out the BOLO on her. Whoever did this, brought the body here in a small tarp, but she wasn't covered very well. I'm surprised it took all day for someone to find her. I guess not many of the residents throw out trash on weekends."

"She had her throat cut?" I asked.

"Yep, cause of death, she bled out, but where? I'm sure it will come out eventually."

"So, how's it feel to be off the murder team, Lynn running solo now?" I asked.

"It feels wrong, but it's good to know I don't have to worry about who the killer is now, Lynn can handle it alone," Deacon replied.

"Has she said anything about it yet?"

"Nope, I think it's good that we aren't arguing about our feelings as to who and how the murder came about. She's a strong woman, she has her own opinions and I have mine. We just weren't good working together, then taking our work home with us. All is good now," he said with a happy smile on his face.

"Sex is good now too?" I asked quietly.

"Oh yeah," he replied with a slight blush. I laughed.

Lynn came over to us, "Well, we don't have much until Joe does the autopsy and forensics checks everything out, but I don't think we are going to get much from here. She still could have set up the murder of Ricky by someone else, but that person decided to take her out too."

Penny said, "She did it, I'm sure."

"You're really hoping it was her for Ricky's murder; just don't want to lose the bet, eh?" I said.

"Hey, twenty is twenty, besides, I don't like to lose," Penny replied.

Lynn turned when she heard her name called by Joe Lang, she went to him. We watched Lynn leaned down to Joe, still at the body as he handed her one of those evidence bags with what looked like a small piece of paper in it. She stood up and was studying the paper, then came back to us.

"I guess whoever murdered her didn't check all her pockets. Joe found this in that little watch pocket that some jeans still have, you know the one above the regular front pocket. It's an unsigned note, all it says is, 'I know what you did, meet me in the Monte Carlo parking structure at 11pm.' Nothing more. Okay, I'm still good for Mary Lou for the murder." Lynn gave the evidence bag to a CSI and instructions for it. "There's nothing more here, shall we go search the parking structure?"

Once again we all piled into our vehicles and drove over to the Monte Carlo and around to the parking garage. Lynn stopped out front and told all of us to take different levels and see if we can find anything, blood especially. She had me go up to the second level and Trapper taking the third. I drove up and then slowly drove around the sea of cars watching between them for anything.

My cell phone buzzed, it was Trapper, he said to call Lynn and get everyone up to the third level, he found the crime scene.

*

Chapter 13

I was heading for the up ramp as I saw Lynn's unmarked car beat me from the lower level and zip up the drive. She was in a rush. I followed her and drove around the aisles of cars until I found Trapper's Jeep and Lynn standing by him and Buffy. Deacon was squatting down looking at something on the pavement between two parked cars.

I pulled into a vacant spot; Penny and I got out and went over to the others. As I approached, I could see the dark red stain on the cement looking like it had dried up without being cleaned. I was sure everyone who parked in the structure ignored the mess; they wanted to get down with gambling and spending their hard-earned cash, a pool of blood wasn't their concern. Maybe they figured it was some poor slob who lost all his life savings and committed suicide. But we knew better.

"Well, there's no blood splatter on the cars, so they weren't here when this happened," Lynn said. "Someone slit her throat, let her lay long enough to get a tarp open to wrap her in it, causing less blood spill here but enough to make this the scene of the crime. Then he or she took Mary Lou to the dumpster and disposed of her."

"I'd say it was a van, easier to put her in the tarp and carry her out. Think you may be able to get something on the surveillance cameras?" I asked.

Honky Tonk Murders

We looked around and the cameras were all facing different directions, none aimed at the crime scene.

"Whoever did this, knew where the cameras were. We may be able to get a sighting on the vehicle from the cameras on the ramps. If we can get an exact time on the killing, I'll call Joe Lang and see what he has. Warren and Williams can dig through the casino videos to see what they can come up with. I've got to call CSI and get them out here." She went off and made her call.

Deacon came to us and said, "There's not a lot of blood, but enough for her to have started to bleed out. The rest has to be in the vehicle because the tarp wasn't bloody enough. She wasn't wrapped very tightly, it was sloppy. Like maybe a woman may have done this."

"Now that's rather sexist, Deacon," Penny said.

"I'm just basing it on past cases; men tend to be more methodical and careful. Women tend to rush into it and get sloppy. Just from what I've seen," Deacon said.

"So what other woman could have done it, there's the waitress, Linda, the only other woman who could have been hurt by Ricky. Maybe she saw or knew Mary Lou had something to do with Ricky's death. Can you run a search on her to see what she drives?" I asked.

Lynn came back, Deacon explained about Linda, she went to her car and did a LEIN search on the waitress from information she had from prior interviews. She waited as the electronic box did it's magic and then came back with the findings. Linda drove a van.

"I just don't know, the throat slash was clean and quick, could Linda have had the ability to do it?" Lynn asked.

"I watched Linda cut up lemons and limes for drinks at the bar. The knife was small and very sharp, she seems to know how to wield a knife, she could have used that," Penny added. "It was small enough to carry and very sharp, but I wonder if Mary Lou would have let her get close enough to slit her throat?"

"True, I'll have her looked into and see what her van reveals before she can clean it out, if she hasn't already," Lynn said. "Who had bets on Linda being the killer?"

Trapper sheepishly raised his hand, Lynn said, "Of course you would. Jim, you haven't said who you want in this sordid little murder?"

"I'm not sure, there are too many reasons everyone had for doing him in. We don't really have much on anybody to go by. But if I had to say who did it, I'd go with Jenny out in Arizona." I held up my arm to protect me from the whacking I was about to get from Penny, but she held back, I was surprised. I put my arm down and then she gave me a good shot to my arm causing me to wince in pain, she had a mean right when she wanted it.

"Okay, we don't have much more to go on, I'm tired and as soon as forensics get here, I may call it a night. Unless one of you has a better idea."

We all agreed, it was now after midnight and I was feeling the day. We said our good-byes, Penny and I went off to the van and I drove home. Willy was sleeping in the kitchen when we came in, he barely moved for us. I hoped he was all right.

Penny went right for the pool, to take a late night swim, that perked Willy up as he joined her. I just sat by the poolside thinking about the case. Who had the most to gain from Ricky's death? Money, love, jealousy and revenge were usually the motives for murder, so what one or two did Ricky bring out in someone enough to kill.

There was Buster, faithful sidekick on the road to fame in music land, but he didn't like Ricky's lifestyle, and how he treated Jenny. Maybe he had a thing for Jenny and wanted Ricky out of the way. But why kill the golden goose of their band's future fame. Maybe Ricky was going to go solo and drop the band. That would also make Buster angry.

Geech? Well he didn't like Ricky's lifestyle either, but was he annoyed enough to murder. Then there was the new kid on the block, hey, where have I heard that name before? Could Jerry have bumped off Ricky to take his place, but it wouldn't have been a good move if Jerry didn't have the talent to fill Ricky's cowboy boots.

On the other side, women. Now that could be where murder may have come from. Mary Lou, the unsuspecting second wife, could she have found out about the Arizona wife? She also wasn't happy with the money Ricky was spending of hers, a quickie divorce and out of the problem. Linda was promised that Ricky would marry her when he got rid of Mary Lou, could she have been mad enough to do Ricky in, but wait, wouldn't she murder Mary Lou first before Ricky? Makes no sense there if she did it. Perhaps Mary Lou did murder Ricky and Linda found out, could she have killed Mary Lou out of revenge.

Can't leave out Jenny in Arizona, she would have had the most to gain, she could have found out about Ricky's second wife and figured with his insurance, she would have had two problems solved, Ricky and wealth. I don't think Penny would have liked knowing that her cousin was a murderess. But she couldn't do it directly, she would have had to hire someone to put him down. My head was starting to hurt with possibilities, besides Penny looked so good swimming in the pool naked. She was in such a hurry to get in, she bypassed the swimsuit.

What the hell, I wasn't going to drown. I stood, stripped off my clothes and slipped in quietly before Penny knew what I was doing. I came up behind her talking to Willy and swam down between her legs causing her to scream. I came up on the front side of her as she had an expression on her face of sheer terror.

I laughed but I was close enough for her to hit me. Then she laughed and attacked me. We flopped around in the water as Willy was floating nearby, probably wondering what his crazy owners were doing.

We finally left the pool and our wet love-making and dried each other off. I was glad that Angelo hadn't came in the backyard while we indulged our lust. I was still amazed that for two sixty-something year olds, we still had it in the sex department.

Honky Tonk Murders

"You're evil, you know that. I never thought that you'd come in and when you swam under me, it frightened the hell out of me. I could have had a heart attack you know," Penny said drying her hair.

"I think you would have murdered me first before having an attack. I was prepared for an assault from you, thankfully you didn't have your .38 nearby."

"It was in my purse, close enough to have gotten it if I hadn't seen it was you."

I looked over and saw her purse at the edge of the pool, I guess she could have.

My cell phone buzzed on the ground where it slipped out of my pants when I dropped them. Willy was barking at the buzzing phone as I picked it up and saw it was Lynn.

"It's too late to go anywhere else, I hope you don't have another body?" I said as I answered.

"Nope, but I sent a couple men over to the bar to check out Linda's van. But she didn't have it, she says it was stolen two nights ago. She says she reported it to the police, but I called the precinct and they can't find the report, so she just moved up my list of suspects on Mary Lou's murder. I really hate double homicides."

*

Chapter 14

I told Penny what Lynn said, "Trapper will love this, he thinks Linda did it, but I'm not convinced. I'm sure when Lynn checks Linda's alibi for the night of Mary Lou's murder, she'll find that she worked that night. We were there, remember? I don't recall her ever leaving the bar, so I'm pretty sure Linda didn't kill Mary Lou."

"You're just a spoilsport aren't you?" Penny smiled.

"I just like justice to be served to the right people. Now who may have taken Linda's van and I wonder if they'll find it," I said.

"Who wasn't in the bar that night?" Penny asked.

I had to think a minute, my brain cells were getting worse now, so my long-term memory was becoming fragmented. My short-term memory wasn't much better, I hated getting old.

"Well, the last day we saw Mary Lou alive, the entire band was off, but Linda was working. So this turns things around again. I wonder how close Linda was to the band."

"You think one of them could have taken her van and used it for the kill on Mary Lou?"

"It's possible, they need to find the van first to be able to tell. I'm done in for the night; shall we turn our brains off and go to bed?" I said.

"You can turn your brain off, but can you turn off the rest of your body?" Penny said with a big grin.

"Especially around your groin."

"Hey, I had enough sex for the night in the pool, you're lucky I even got into the water."

"Bull, you just like seeing me naked," she said and dropped the towel wrapped around her, exposing her naked body again as she ran into the house, Willy running behind her. I followed them.

We were snuggling in bed, not indulging in sex, just comfy together. Penny whispered to me, "I still think Mary Lou did it, and she was killed by one of the band who was bent on revenge for Ricky's murder."

"Would make a good story, but I don't know if Mary Lou would have done it, she didn't seem to know much about Ricky's personal life other than he was spending her money on frivolous things."

"Just my point, she resented his spending and did him in." Penny said with a kiss to my cheek.

"Seems it would be simpler to just cut him off from any more money. Murder is so final and if Ricky's records were gaining on the charts, she would be cutting off any return on her investment. I don't think she knew about Jenny in Arizona, she seemed genuinely surprised when I mentioned it. So she really didn't have a motive for murder. Now Buster didn't like what Ricky was doing to Jenny, he may have motive for murder if he thought he was doing good for her," I said returning the kiss.

"Sure, I see it now, Buster had a big crush on Jenny and did Ricky in to open the way to her," Penny said excitedly. "A typical love triangle."

"Sure and now Jenny is worth millions, he'd get

that too. If he can prevent anyone from finding out he murdered Ricky."

"So he kills Mary Lou to make it look like she did it."

"That doesn't compute, if Mary Lou didn't do it, why would he want her dead? He would need to prove she did it and not kill her. He'd have to set her up for the murder to take the attention away from him."

"I'm getting a headache, I don't know how you can do all these deductions to find a killer. I'm leaving it up to you now." She turned with her back to me, spooning.

I still had my arms around her until she was asleep. I let her slip to her side of the bed and I turned on my side facing the bed table where my Glock, cell phone and the alarm clock rested. I always made sure the gun was close at hand, but kept it on safety so I didn't accidently shoot Penny in my sleep.

I lay there for a while thinking about the people all involved in the case, not really finding any common thread, but everyone had a motive in one way or another. Maybe they all did it, one of those murder pacts and each one put poison in his drink. There, we could now go arrest everyone and the case is closed. I realized that I was getting loopy, so tried to go to sleep.

The next noise I heard was Penny yelling to me to get up; we had criminals to apprehend. I opened one eye and saw her at her closet pulling clothes out and throwing them on the bed over my feet. I struggled to get up, my body creaking and groaning as it moved all the bones back into place.

Sunday mornings were supposed to be quiet times having a nice breakfast, hopefully made by Angelo, and relaxing. I had a feeling that this was not going to be one of those mornings by watching Penny getting ready to attack the day.

"What's got you all raring to go so early?" I asked.

"I have an obligation to my cousin to catch her husband's killer, and we will do so. Now get up and get moving." She took her clothes for the day and left the bedroom on her way to her bathroom. I stood slowly allowing my body to stretch into some form of human. I went to my bathroom out in the hallway, Penny took command of the bath in the bedroom, so I had to traipse out in the hall to get to mine.

I did my morning ritual of ogling my image in the mirror, wishing for plastic surgery on a few parts of my physique and wondering if I should dye my beard and mustache, killing the grey. It might make me look younger, but wouldn't help the aging process. I finished up in the bathroom and threw on some clothes, then headed for the kitchen where I found our faithful friend Angelo whipping up some delightful breakfast.

"Good morning Mr. R., how'd you sleep?" the big man asked.

"Lousy, thank you Angelo. Are you off to guard anyone today?"

"Yep the big country awards is tonight and I have to keep my client safe up to the show."

"Any one we know?

"Nah, she's no Reba or Shania, just some new

singer up for the breakout artist award. Her managers wanted to be sure some overzealous fan didn't hurt her, so I'm protecting her today."

"Well, she's in good hands." I sat at the snack counter as Penny put a plate of what looked strangely like Army SOS in front of me. "Ah, good old 'shit on a shingle'. I haven't had this since I was in the Army." Referring to the gravy covered biscuit.

"Yeah, my mother used to serve it to us once a week and I got a fondness for it. I figured you'd remember it," Angelo laughed,

We ate our breakfast and then Angelo went off to get ready for his day. I pulled my cell phone and called Lynn.

"Any new developments since last night?" I asked when she answered.

"Good morning to you too," she replied. "Nothing dramatic, still looking for Linda's van, no luck so far. It could be out of the state by now."

"Or in the desert," I said.

"We got a spotter plane searching for that aspect. Still nothing."

"Hate to spoil your day but Linda has an alibi for the night of Mary Lou's murder."

"What?"

"Penny and me, we were with her in the bar around the time Mary Lou was being slit. So that rules her out. Now the band wasn't there so they still can be in the running," I said as I took the last bite of my gravy biscuit.

"You always have an answer don't you?"

"That's why I'm the P.I. and you're not," I said with a laugh.

"You call yourself a private investigator, ha."

"Hey, I've saved Vegas from terrorists and dirty bombs. I get to be hero once in a while."

"I'll see that you get the key to the city, where do we go now Sherlock?"

"I think I'd like to do a little more talking to Buster and Geech, we didn't have much of a heart to heart with them."

"I'll get an address of where they are staying from our files from when we did talk to them, and yes, we didn't really have a heart to heart with them, sound like a winner."

"Shall we meet you at the precinct or will you call with the address?"

"I'll call, so finish your breakfast and wait." She hung up. I finished my breakfast.

About fifteen minutes later she called and gave me the address of the motel they were staying at. It was the same one that Lacey was involved with a murder at when we first met her, so I knew exactly where it was.

Penny and I gathered our things and Penny picked up Willy who was still licking up the plate of gravy Angelo gave him. She put him in his travel bag and slung him over her shoulder.

"Willy needs some time outside with us," she said as we went out to the van. I drove over to the Vegas boulevard and up to the motel. I pulled in just as I saw Lynn and Deacon standing outside the main office. I parked in the side lot.

"Deacon, are you slumming today?" I asked as we approached.

"Vice is a little slow, so I'm tagging along to be sure Lynn doesn't get hurt," he laughed.

"Funny, the day I need your help… " her voice trailed off. "Well I'll be damned." She was looking towards the corner of the motel parking lot, where there was a white van parked. "Plates match, we found our missing murder van."

*

Chapter 15

We went to the van, "Don't touch the thing until I get CSI here," Lynn said.

We walked around it and could see blood splatter on the left rear tire well. We had our crime vehicle.

"Why would they just leave the thing sitting here so close to their room?" Deacon wondered.

"Maybe we're dealing with stupid people?" I joked.

"This is too easy; I'm wondering if it could be a set up?" Lynn said.

Lynn took a rubber glove out of her back pocket; I wondered what all she carried in her clothes. She snapped on the glove and opened the side sliding door. We all peered in and could see there was a good amount of blood on the floor. To one side were a couple of tarps.

"I wonder what Linda was doing with all the tarps?" I said. "Does she have a business on the side?"

"I'll be sure to ask her, once we get results from this?" Lynn replied.

"You think this could be anyone else's blood?" Penny asked.

"No, I'm sure this came from Mary Lou, but if I go accusing without proof, I may blow the whole thing. I'm not going to mess this up, that's Deacon's job," she said with a laugh.

"Hey, I resent that. I've never blown a case," Deacon defended.

We turned to see the CSI Explorer pulling into the parking lot. Lynn waved them over and they parked, jumped out and after conferring with Lynn got on the van. Lynn said, "Time to go question the band."

We went to the office and in to find the same older woman who we questioned back when we were investigating the Sin City murders. She got a look on her face saying that she remembered us or she had constipation, either way she didn't look happy.

"Hi, since you seem to recognize us, we need to know what room Buster Jones or Geech Goodwin are in," Lynn asked.

She just sighed and went into her register, looked through it and just said, "Room 12, and don't go shooting up the place."

"Thanks, we'll try not to," Lynn said and led us out. We went to the room and stood back as Lynn knocked on the door. She did it again after a few minutes then the door opened with a very sleepy looking Buster in his tighty whities.

"What now?" he grumbled.

"Just need to talk to you again about a new murder, can you put some pants on please."

"Why? I'm comfortable, and you are intruding on my sleep."

"Well, you could let us talk here or we can take you to our station in your underwear and question you there," Lynn said with a grin.

Buster looked at the small mob of people outside and snorted, "Fine, come in and I'll dress for the occasion. But do all these people need to be in here?"

Lynn looked to us, turned back to Buster and said, "They're all part of the investigation."

"Whatever." He turned and went back into the room; it was a mess, beer cans and papers all over the place. On one of the beds, Geech was sprawled out sound asleep. Buster pulled on a pair of pants and gave Geech a push off the bed. Geech came up ready to fight and saw us.

"What the hell, what is this?" he said with a drunken slur.

Buster said, "Cool your jets, we are being requested to talk to the police, now be nice or go to jail."

Geech got meek and sat on the end of the bed. Buster picked up a pack of cigarettes and lit one. He came to us and said, "Now what do we owe the pleasure of this visit?"

"You knew Mary Lou, Ricky's second wife?" Lynn asked.

"Well of course. I told you I didn't like Ricky marrying her."

"Did you not like her enough to murder her?"

"What the hell you talking about, what murder?"

"Mary Lou was found dead last night and we found the van she was transported in, it's right here in your parking lot. CSI is examining it right now." She pointed out the open door to where the forensic techs were examining the van.

"Van? You talking about Linda's van? We used it to move equipment yesterday and returned it to the bar, where Linda was at. I don't know about any other use it got or how it got back here."

"So you're saying Linda knew you had the van?"

"That's right, she let us use it a couple times to move our stuff when we had to change steel guitar players. We had it yesterday early and took it back to her."

"Well, she says it was stolen a couple days ago and now it's out in your parking lot."

Buster turned to Geech, "Didn't Linda let us use the van?"

Geech was being quiet and just nodded. Then he said, "She did that, she did."

Lynn looked to Deacon and me and said, "This is getting complicated. Someone is lying and I think it's Linda." She turned back to Buster, "So you had the van early yesterday and returned it to her at the bar. Did you give her the keys personally or what?"

"Well no, she always had the keys in the van so we could just take it when we needed it. Ricky made a fuss about marrying her so he could get her to let us use it."

I whispered to Penny, "Seems like Ricky used marriage a lot to get what he wanted from women." She whacked my arm.

Lynn asked Buster, "Did Linda see you return the van yesterday?"

Buster thought a bit then said, "Well, no she didn't. We dropped it off and left in my car to come back here. Actually, I don't even know if she was working when we returned it. I just figured she was."

"So it's possible that she didn't know you had the van?"

"Uh, yeah I guess. We got the thing day before yesterday and moved the equipment then returned it yesterday. Okay Linda didn't see us take the thing or return it, so I guess she could have thought it was stolen. She told Ricky that we could take it any time we needed it."

"I guess it's a matter of crossed signals, but that doesn't explain how it got back here or the blood all over it. Do you have any ideas about that?"

"Hell no, I already said I don't know how the van got back here or that Mary Lou was killed. Geech and I've been together for the last three days, without no breaks, so he's my alibi and I'm his."

I could tell Lynn was getting frustrated, "Do you know any reason why someone would kill Mary Lou?" I asked Buster.

"Hell, the only person I knew who'd kill Mary Lou

was Ricky, he was getting real fed up with her, he regretted marrying her something fierce. But him doing it is not possible now."

"I'd say so," Lynn said and then, "Thanks for your time, go back to sleep and we'll talk later, maybe."

She turned and headed out the door. I looked to Deacon and he just shrugged and followed. I smiled to Buster and led Penny with Willy out to follow our friends. Lynn was standing just away from the CSI still tearing apart the van with her hands on her hips, looking in deep thought. We came up and she said, "I certainly hope they find something."

"You know they'll find fingerprints all over the thing from Buster, Geech, Linda and probably Ricky," I said.

"Yeah, I know, but I'm hoping there may be something else that we can go with. I'm not going to worry about it until they find something. I think we need to talk to Linda to get her story on this van lending business. We really should pull everyone into the station and put them all in one room and beat the hell out of them. This doesn't help my love for country music."

"I didn't know you liked country," Deacon said.

"I just don't go around singing it," Lynn replied.

"Actually I've never ever heard you sing at all," Deacon came back.

"You really don't want to hear me sing," she said and walked away towards her car. Deacon just looked lost and I said to follow her or be left behind. He ran after her.

I turned to my favorite girl with dog and said, "I

think Lynn is very distracted, wouldn't you say?"

Penny looked like she was struggling with a thought, "I probably shouldn't tell you this, and if you tell Deacon, I'll kill you!"

"Please don't tell me Lynn is going to leave him?"

"No worse, Lynn is pregnant," Penny announced.

I just stood with my mouth open. "Close your mouth Sweetie, it's not something she's happy about, well, actually she is but it means that she may have to step aside from her job when she starts showing."

"They didn't practice safe sex?"

"Hell, when was the last time we practiced safe sex?" Penny laughed.

"But we're past having children… aren't we?"

"I've heard of women having children in later years, but if you remember I told you after we met, I can't get pregnant, due to internal problems. But Lynn is still healthy and young. She's happy, but not sure of her future as a cop."

"Nine months of carrying around the extra weight and then maternity leave, maybe she'll get a desk job on the force."

"Lynn behind a desk, I don't think so."

I just watched Lynn and Deacon drive off, and was totally amazed.

*

Chapter 16

After we went back home to change into evening clothes we drove out to the MGM Grand where they were having the CMA awards show. I told Lynn we were going to check it out and she got us free passes to the main show. We arrived and parked, the show was being telecast around five in the afternoon so it would go out to the east coast by eight in the evening. I wasn't fond of the time zones but it was something you couldn't change.

I saw a good number of country stars, even though I didn't admit that I liked country, I actually did. My favorites were Shania Twain, Jennifer Nettles from Sugarland and Faith Hill. Of course they were all totally beautiful women, it didn't matter to me. I just never told Penny, who could outdo any of them for beauty. But I was prejudiced in her favor.

We passed Angelo in the main lobby of the hotel before we entered the auditorium to the show. He was looking officious and had on his blazer identifying him as a member of the Richard's Investigations and Security. I had to agree with Buck that getting the embroidery on the pocket was a good idea. Angelo saw us and gave a quick wave, then gave his attention back to the attractive woman he was escorting. People were trying to get near her, but Angelo kept them at arm's length. I was happy for my friend that he got out of the life as a mob enforcer and into a job that he enjoyed.

He and his charge went into the auditorium and disappeared in the crowd. I led Penny into the huge concert venue and looked to the tickets for seating numbers that Lynn provided us. Police have a way of getting perks for things like this. Either the concert people cough up tickets or face inspectors looking to close down the place with safety infractions. It was a give and take world.

We found our seats, they were in the middle section but about a thousand rows back or so it seemed. I looked at the sea of people between the stage and us, remembering years back when I saw Frank Sinatra in an outdoor concert. The people I was with had tickets to the lawn seating back up on a hill, no chairs, just a square patch of grass to spread a blanket out on. When Sinatra came out, he looked like he was about one inch tall. The speakers were effective and we enjoyed the concert, but he was so far away they could have put a mannequin on stage and played a recording, it wouldn't have made any difference.

I liked the fact that our seats were on the aisle, I hated climbing over people, but on the other hand, people would be climbing over me now. I looked to the seats next to us and there were four open seats, I wondered who would be sitting there. As I was thinking about it, I felt a presence standing next to me and looked up to see a smiling Lynn Carter with Deacon behind her. I stood and moved out to the aisle.

"We would have been here sooner but Deacon takes so long getting cleaned up," Lynn said with a smile as she and Deacon climbed over Penny to get to the seats next to us.

"Why didn't you tell us you were coming?" Penny asked.

"I thought it would be fun to surprise you," she said and sat next to Penny.

"Am I going to regret asking who the next two seats are for?" I asked.

"You'll see," she said with an evil grin.

I figured it would be Trapper with a date and I was right as I saw him and Buffy coming up the aisle towards us. He stood grinning and I got up again.

"You couldn't get here with the rest of us?" I said.

"What, and spoil my entrance?" he said as they climbed over Penny, Lynn and Deacon to their seats.

"I looked down the row and said, "I hope no one has to use the bathroom anytime soon."

Lynn smiled and said, "Only when your favorite acts are on."

The auditorium lights flashed and I could see the camera crews scrambling to get in position. The announcer came over the P.A. and did his intro and the show started. We could see the action on the big jumbo screens they had set up for us people out in the back forty.

The show went well, very enjoyable. I got to see all my favorite female singers, I just wished I had binoculars so I could see them better. Although looking through binoculars would have been just like watching them on TV, we needed closer seats. I'd have to talk to Lynn about better seats for the next show.

We endured two and a half hours of the show, complete with commercial breaks, but it was interesting to see how they would break down the set for each act. They had good stage hands to move all the equipment. They also had a revolving stage so they could move one band off and another on.

Finally all the awards were given out and the singers sang, the show ended. I had a better appreciation for television and how they kept everything in perspective with all the different cameras around the room. It was a well choreographed ballet of cameramen and grips all moving cables and equipment around the audience and the performers on stage.

I stood as everyone in the auditorium did. This was the one thing I really hated, the end of a show with the audience fighting to get to their cars. I looked back to my troop of crime fighters and announced, "We are going to the one of the restaurants here for a dinner, on me."

They all liked the idea of me paying and also not having to fight the traffic going out of the parking structure. We went to the lobby and over to where they had all the various food services and I led everyone to the buffet line.

"I knew you'd be cheap and get us into the buffet," Penny said.

"I happen to think their buffet is excellent," I replied.

"If you like eating in a cafeteria," Trapper spoke.

"You keep out of this, free show and free food, you have nothing to complain about," I said to him as he just grinned back at me.

We had eaten and the crowd had dissipated, so getting to our cars would be a lot easier now. We sat at our table relaxing before heading out.

"Are you still going to take Ricky's body back to Arizona?" Lynn asked me.

"As soon as we can get him out of the morgue and to the mortuary for cremation. I need to call Jenny and fill her in on what's happening and find out if she made arrangements out there."

"I'll call Joe Lang and see if he can speed up the process. Call Hannigan and arrange with him to call Joe also," Lynn said.

"Hannigan said he'd take care of it as soon as I give him the go ahead," I replied.

"Are you driving him to Phoenix?" Trapper asked.

"That's the plan, it will be a nice little vacation in the van and we'll get to see the mountains in Arizona. I looked at a map and routed a scenic tour to Bullhead City then over to Flagstaff, Arizona and finally off the main highway down through the Mazatzal Mountain range, sightseeing along the way. It should be a nice ride."

"I just think it's creepy to carry a departed person in a vehicle other than a hearse," Trapper grinned as he said this.

"He'll be going first class, I'll strap him to the passenger seat. Well, I'll strap his urn to it."

"You can put him outside at night while we sleep too," Penny said. "I'm not sleeping with a dead body so close in the van."

"Oh sure and we wake up the next morning to find that raccoons have opened up his urn and spread the ashes all over the place," I laughed.

"Would that be so bad?" she said. "Save jenny from spreading them."

"Whatever, we'll see what happens. Now I'm ready to depart," I said and looked to Lynn. "Shall we go see what Linda has to say?"

"I still don't have much help from forensics other than the blood was from Mary Lou, but we figured that. There were fingerprints all over the van and most matched up to the band. There are two that aren't in the system, so they are still running them. I'd like to find out about the lending of the van and why Linda said she reported the theft, I couldn't find anything in the computers."

We finished and went out to our vehicles. The traffic had lessened from the parking structure and I drove out to Shindigs and parked in the back lot. Penny and I waited for Lynn and Trapper to arrive, and sat talking about the show.

About five minutes later, they pulled in and parked. We all went into the building and found a table by the dance floor. I didn't see Linda working, just the brunette we met the first night we were in here. She came over and asked for our drink order. Everyone told her what they wanted and she went off to get them. About five minutes later she returned and gave everyone their drinks.

"Can you tell me if Linda is working tonight?" I asked.

"Linda never showed up for work, we called her but no answer so we had to call in a replacement."

I looked to Lynn as she said, "I think we need to go visit Linda at home, just to make sure she's alive."

*

Chapter 17

Lynn made a phone call to the precinct to get Linda's home address. She waited as someone who answered the call did a check on a computer and gave Lynn the info she needed. By this time we had finished up our drinks and left before the band started to play.

We were out in the parking lot when a thought came to me. I stopped Lynn and asked, "I just thought about the big S-20 pick-up truck that Ricky had, why would they have needed Linda's van to move anything in the past as Buster said? He told us that Ricky asked Linda if they could use the van, why?"

"Now there's a point I didn't think of either, we really need to get Linda and the band in and question them. This is becoming too loose of a case."

"Why don't you go check on Linda and I'll go talk to Buster about this," I said. Lynn agreed and went off followed by Trapper and Buffy. I took Penny back into the bar and went over to where Buster and Geech were sitting at a table. He saw me and got an annoyed look.

I came up and sat on a chair next to him as Penny sat at the table next to me. "Buster, I have a few more questions to ask. All we're trying to do is find out who killed Ricky, so I hope you will be cooperative."

"Hey, I want to find out who did it too, so ask your questions," he said sounding more friendly now.

"Good, now you told us earlier that Ricky asked Linda if you guys could use her van to move equipment, but Ricky had the pick-up truck, why didn't you use that to move?"

"Timing was wrong, Ricky said he had things to do with the truck and he asked Linda if Geech and I could use the van for moving the steel guitar player's equipment, besides Ricky wasn't happy about other people driving his truck. So we ended up using the van."

I thought that made some sense, "Do you know where Linda is this evening, she seems to be missing?"

"Nope, I haven't any idea where she is, I'm not interested in her to keep track. That was Ricky's job."

"You didn't like Ricky's fooling around did you?"

"I am a faithful man to one woman, if I had one. I didn't approve of Ricky dallying around with women. Every town we were in he would pick up some woman to use for the time we were there. I felt sorry for Jenny but it wasn't my business to stick my nose in."

"Were any of these women mad enough at him for his fooling around?"

"Hell, he made sure they didn't know, he was good at that, he was a right good liar when he had to be."

I glanced over to Penny, she didn't look happy.

I asked, "So if you had to make a decision as to who the killer might be, who would you say?"

He sat back in his chair looking like he was sorting through his mind, "I don't know, I would have said Mary Lou, she was mean enough, but who killed her? You got a tough case here."

"Yes, we do, but we will find out who did it, I promised Jenny I would. Thanks for your help, I'm sure Lieutenant Carter will have some more questions later. She's out looking for Linda now." I stood and took Penny out to the van.

I pulled my cell phone and called Deacon, I didn't want to disturb Lynn. He came on after a couple rings and I asked if they found Linda.

"The house was empty, no sign of her. Lynn put out a BOLO, hopefully we don't find her in a dumpster," Deacon said.

"Ricky is dead, followed by Mary Lou, now Linda is missing. Is someone covering their tracks on this? Or has Linda flown the coop as the killer. Her van was used, she didn't like Ricky being married to Mary Lou and stringing her along. Love can be a killer."

"Yeah, I love Lynn but lately I feel like murdering her, she has gotten so damn moody."

"Deacon, don't ask questions, and just be patient with her, I'm sure everything will be explained soon,"

I said hoping he would take it at that and drop it.

"Patient? What's there to be patient about?" he asked with a slight tremor in his voice, "Is she going to dump me?"

"Deacon! No, just don't think about it, you'll know when the time is right." Now I was needing to shut up. "Deacon call me when you find Linda and don't say anything to Lynn, you hear me." I hung up and sat there feeling like I just gave up the top-secret plans to attack Iran.

"Smooth move, slick," Penny said to me, "That's going to last about two minutes before Deacon interrogates Lynn. I'd say you better stay away from her for a day or two."

My cell phone buzzed and I looked at the caller ID, it was Lynn. "Damn, he didn't even wait two minutes, should I answer?"

"If you don't, she'll track you down."

I pushed the answer button with regret, "Hello?"

"Jim, Lynn here, did you talk to Buster?" she said calmly.

"Uh, yeah… everything alright on your end?" I asked.

"Sure, why wouldn't it be?"

"Nothing, I did talk to Buster and I don't believe he had anything to do with the crime, but I have been wrong before."

"Oh yes you have, but you have been right more times. We're going home, it's been a long day and I hope in the morning they have Linda in custody. I'm still going to bring in Buster and Geech for questioning. So if you want to be in on the interrogation, call in the morning," she said and hung up.

I sat taking in a breath.

"Bit the bullet for now did you?" Penny said.

I started the van and grinned to her. I drove home.

We got back and Penny went in as I parked the van. I came into the kitchen to find Penny feeding Willy who was bouncing around her feet. I watched the two of them just as I heard a knock on the side door. I peeked through the hole in the door and saw it was Angelo.

I opened the door and said, "Hey big guy, what's up?"

"I saw youse guys pulling in and wanted to say hello and tell you that my night was good. No trouble or stupid fans," he said with a smile.

"Angelo that's great, you got your client safely back to her hotel?"

"Sure did, and she wanted to have me come in for a few drinks, but I figured what she wanted, I declined."

"Was she upset?"

"Well she wasn't happy, but her manager came by and she pulled him into her room and I was safe," he laughed. "How you doing on your case?"

"A confusing mess, so far. We have too many suspects and so little evidence. But I'm not going to kill myself, this is Lynn's case and I'm just trying to help," I said.

"Don't forget, you told my cousin that you'd catch the killer," Penny piped up.

"Yes dear, I think I did say that and I'm going to do my best. Angelo, do you have anything coming up now?" I said trying to change the subject.

"Nah, I'm taking a few days off to do a little sightseeing around the Vegas Valley, I'd like to drive up to Mt. Charleston and over to the Hoover Dam."

"Well, that sounds good, but it may take more than a few days to do all that, why don't you take a week and I'll have Buck give you a bonus in your pay to help with your trip."

"Gee, Mr. R, that would be real nice, thank you. Well I'll let you two get to bed, I'm a bit worn out myself from following my client around that huge building," he said and went out after we all said our goodnights.

Willy was still munching on his food when Penny and I slipped quietly to our bedroom. We were in bed and snuggling before the dog even missed us. He wasn't happy to find us starting ahead of him. He went to his Bate's Motel chair that we bought for him during the Magic Murders and he just huffed, then spun a few times flopping down. He was asleep before we were.

"Are you going to get Ricky cremated and back home before you solve the case here?" Penny asked in my ear.

"Well, once he's ashes it won't matter, he won't decompose after that, so no rush. I'd like to tie up the loose ends here, but maybe we need the trip out to Phoenix for a little diversion. I'll see how the next couple days go before making a decision."

"I'll need to get some time off from the show if you go during the week," Penny said.

"I think we can wait till next weekend for the trip; that will give me time to do some more investigating."

"I wonder where Linda is now. I hope we don't find her dead also," Penny said with a yawn, sounding sleepy.

"Get some sleep and we'll worry about it in the morning."

"I have to go back to the studio tomorrow; Mondays are not my favorite day."

"But you love your job."

"I do, but I want to find out who did the crime."

"As soon as I find out I'll call you," I said and she didn't answer. I look to her and she was sound asleep, I wish I could pass out like that.

*

Chapter 18

I lay there for a long while after she dozed off. Some nights I couldn't get to sleep till almost time to get up, a fifteen minute nap. I turned to face Penny looking so soft and sweet in the bare light from the hallway shining through the open bedroom door. It's amazing how absolutely beautiful a woman can look in slumber. There was something about the face at rest that brings out beauty. Not the hard, harsh mask a person puts on while awake, facing the day and unknown future.

I reached over and traced her face starting with her forehead and down her nose to her lips. I brushed those luscious lips and she smiled. I didn't think I woke her but she must have felt something. I leaned forward and gave her lips a little kiss, she responded but still slept. I hope she was dreaming of me as we kissed.

"Oh Eric, you kiss so well," she murmured.

"Are you going to start that again, I thought we got over the Eric-Pixie thing long ago," I said.

"Sorry, but you dragged me out of my dream and I was lost as to where I was," she said opening her eyes and smiling.

"You are a mean person when you want to be," I said turning on my back. She moved over and up on me.

"Aw Sweetie, you know I love only you. I just bring Eric out to make sure you know that."

"Odd logic, but I think I understand. I shouldn't take you for granted, you can always have Eric."

"And you have Pixie, who I haven't heard from much lately."

"I just about forgotten her, if you hadn't brought it up, I may have finally gotten over her."

"You never had a relationship with her, just the image in your mind of a night on the town watching a stripper dance around a pole to 'Lady' by Styx."

"Yes, she was a vision, enough to give me dreams for a long time to come. But I'm over that now, I'm with you."

"If you were on the road a lot, like Ricky, would you be unfaithful?"

"At great risk to my health, no I wouldn't. But there are men who don't believe in total monogamy. I still contend that humankind was not meant to be monogamous. Cats and dogs do it indiscriminately as do most creatures, so man is not a faithful animal."

"But what about those mate for life creatures like ducks, Gibbon apes, wolves, termites, coyotes, barn owls, beavers, bald eagles, condors, swans... "

"Termites?" I interrupted her list, "How do they know termites are monogamous?"

"Studies, how else?"

"And big research grant money. I'd sit and watch termites mate for a salary," I laughed. "Do they have a little wedding ceremony and every anniversary is wood?"

"Quit making fun, there are a lot of creatures that remain faithful."

"Just not Ricky Lawless. I wonder if Jenny knew about his mistresses and wives?"

"You can ask her when we see her, now go to sleep," she said as she moved off me and turned on her side facing away.

"Now you'll have me dreaming about termites and little wedding cakes made of wood."

I could feel the bed shaking slightly from her muted laughter as I turned to try and sleep. "Do they go on a honeymoon to the woods?" She didn't answer.

I just barely closed my eyes when I felt I was being rousted from my bed. I looked up to see

Trapper, now that was startling.

"What the hell are you doing in my bedroom, am I having a nightmare?" I asked.

"No, you're not dreaming, Penny told me to get you out of bed."

"Damn is it morning already?"

"Yep, seven in the glorious morning. I stopped by to see if you wanted any help today to track down your killer."

"Why? Did someone kill me? Now I know this is a nightmare, and why would you think I want your help?"

"I'm the best you got, now what's the plan?"

"I have no plan until I can get myself out of this bed, and I don't need you to help me get up. Go have breakfast with Penny and I'll be out in a short while."

He laughed and headed out, stopping at the door, "Angelo is making blueberry pancakes, you better hurry."

I sat on the edge of the bed shaking the cobwebs out of my head. I finally stood, stretched and went to my bathroom. About twenty minutes later, I was halfway to facing the day, but now I needed food to fuel myself. I found that as I got older, I needed sustenance.

I went out to find Trapper and Buffy sitting at the snack bar munching on pancakes. Penny was in the kitchen getting some more on her plate, she saw me and smiled. Angelo saw me also and waved.

I sat next to Penny after she sat back down. "Are we opening a restaurant here now?" I said looking to Trapper.

"Hey, I thought we were family," Trapper said between bites of food.

"Yes, and you are the strange uncle, who the police are watching. Good morning Buffy, are you along for the ride?" I said with a grin at the young girl trying to prove to be an insurance investigator.

"I still need to report to my company as to who murdered Ricky, the payments will be held up until I get some info. I don't want to disappoint the widow."

"Well, we'll do our best to resolve that. Will, have you heard if they found Linda yet?"

"I talked to Lynn a bit ago and she said that Linda is off the grid, so far no idea where she is. They're watching all the outgoing points from town and unless she is hitchhiking, she should be caught. If she's not dead somewhere."

"That's what I'm worried about. Did Lynn say she was bringing in Buster and Geech for questioning?"

"Yeah, she said to come in around nine for her interrogations."

Angelo put a plate of pancakes in front of me, I thanked him. "Heard from Earl at all?" I asked.

"He and Paula got back from the mountains last night, he called me this morning to see what was going on. He said he called you, but you didn't answer."

"I have this habit of shutting off my cell phone in my sleep. Must be psychological or to stop annoying calls in the morning. Is he going to be in the office this morning?"

"He said he was. Do we have a good missing wedding groom to give him?" Trapper said with a hearty laugh.

"You know he hates those, they were all he had after he moved out here. I don't know what we got coming in, I haven't talked to Lacey yet. I hate Monday mornings," I said as I finished my pancakes. "I'll go finish getting ready and we can go to the office."

I thanked Angelo and went to get my toys to take, my new Palm LifeDrive, my cell phone, my Swiss army knife, and a couple of extra items that I carried for any occasion. I got my Glock and put it in the holster clipped to my belt then covered it with my jacket. I went back out towards the kitchen and found everyone standing on the front porch.

Trapper spoke, "I'm driving Buffy in and we'll see you in a bit." They went off and I turned to Penny giving her a kiss.

"Have a good day interviewing all the big stars. Do you know who you have on your show today?" I asked.

"No I don't, but I'm sure Gordy will tell me as soon as I get in. Don't get murdered and call me if you find out anything about Linda." She kissed me again, picked up Willy and went to her car in the garage. She drove out and down the road.

I went to turn on the security equipment and went out to the van. As I was tooling down the highway towards the office I was piecing things together in my head about the case. We really didn't have much to go on, just that Ricky was poisoned and had a small army of people who wanted him dead. Mary Lou was the most likely suspect but she's dead now too. The real killer must have done her, but why? Could she have figured out who did it and confronted the killer. The note in her pocket said someone knew what she did, so was this a revenge killing?

My head was starting to hurt so I tried to turn it off. I turned on my CD player in the van and put in an album by Sugarland. Who said I didn't know my country music.

I arrived at the office and parked in the back, going through the back door and waved to the spy camera figuring Lacey was watching. I went by Earl's office since he was in the back and he wasn't there. I stopped by Trapper's and he wasn't there either. Was anyone working today I thought after not finding Buck in his office?

I went through the glass doors to the inner lobby where Lacey ruled, and found everyone standing at her desk. I went up and looked over Trapper's shoulder and saw what everyone was looking at.

Jessie was in Lacey's seat smiling at me. Jessie was the abused nine year old girl who's father was murdered by the vigilante murderer and Penny and I took her into our home until Lacey and Mac got married. They became her foster parents after that.

I smiled back and said, "Jessie, how are you doing?"

*

Chapter 19

She grinned back to me, then jumped up, ran around the desk and latched on to me with a big hug, nearly knocking me over. She had gotten much bigger than when I last saw her.

"Jessie, good to see you, what are you doing here, no school?" I asked.

"Uncle Jim, I'm happy to see you too. School is out for vacation so I talked mom into letting me come for a visit," she said bubbling with joy.

I noticed she referred to Lacey as mom, which was good, she was fitting into being a family.

"Well, we'll have to find you some work to do, you can't just hang around here with all these busy people," I said looking to everyone standing around. "Aren't we busy people?"

"Oh yeah… sure… of course… always busy." Came a chorus from them.

I laughed and told Jessie, "Your first job is supervisor, now get these people to work."

Jessie gave me a salute and turned to them saying, "You heard the boss, get to work."

They all smiled and went back to their offices.

Lacey laughed and said, "Okay now get your supervisor butt back over here and finish your homework."

"Homework? On her vacation? They must have some mean teachers at her school," I said.

Honky Tonk Murders

"They have excellent teachers, Jessie is doing very well with her grades," Lacey answered. "Oh, you got a call from Jenny in Arizona. I told her you'd call back when you got in."

"Strange that she didn't call on Penny's phone. Okay, I'll go call her, thanks. Jessie, work hard but have fun with it," I said and went to my office.

I sat at my new desk and picked up the phone, checking my address book. I dialed Jenny and she came on after three rings. "Jenny, it's Jim. I heard you called."

"Yes, I just wanted to know what was happening with Ricky's return?"

"Well, they are releasing the body and we will have him cremated. Then Penny and I will bring him out over the weekend. Is that good for you?"

"Do I still need the funeral home to do anything?"

"Depends on whether you want to inter his remains in a crypt or keep him at home on the mantle? Have you decided what you want to do with the urn?"

"Oh God, I don't want him on the mantle or in the house at all. I'll talk to the funeral home about a crypt for him."

"Most cemeteries have smaller crypts for urns, they're cheaper also. Check on that and we'll have him to you this weekend. On another matter, there is an insurance investigator here looking into the murder. She will have to report to the company her findings before the company can release the funds. So be patient, for that amount of money they don't want to rush. Do you need any money to help with his interment? I can help with that until you get the insurance settlement."

"That would be real helpful, Ricky used to send back money to help with the bills back here, but since his death the money has about dried up."

"Okay, hang in till this weekend and I'll help you out for now. I'll call by Friday to let you know what is happening. How's your daughter?"

"She's better now, the doctors have her stabilized and she can come home soon. It will be a welcome relief to get away from the hospital."

"I can understand; I'll talk to you later then." We said our good-byes and I hung up. I sat thinking about what the day was shaping up to be. I had to go to Metro for the official interrogation of Buster and Geech, so that will take my mind off Ricky's cremation.

My phone rang and I picked it up, "Hello?"

"Jim, this is Joe Lang, thought I would give you a personal call to say the body needs to be picked up by Hannigan as he is scheduled to be cremated, but you have to come in and sign some release papers, can you swing by and take care of that?"

"I have to go to Metro by nine so I can leave early and stop, thanks for the heads up. See you soon." We said our good-byes and I thought my day is getting busy.

I went to Trapper's office and found Buffy sitting in his client chair, but no Trapper. "Where's Mr. Wonderful?"

"He went to get some coffee. Are you going to the interrogation today?"

"Wouldn't miss it. Are you formulating any reports to your company yet? I just talked to the widow and told her I had no answers for her."

"I still don't have concrete proof of his death being committed by anyone other than the beneficiary; I hope we can close this up soon."

"We're doing all we can, the investigation process doesn't solve itself in an hour like on TV, unfortunately. Keep close to Will, he's an ex-cop and a good investigator, he'll help you."

Trapper came back in with two cups of coffee and gave me a big grin. "Are you ready to start your day with a good old-fashion flogging of suspects?"

"We never flog, maybe a little knuckle breaking, but no flogging. I have to stop by the morgue to sign out Ricky's body so I'll see you at Metro later." I left and went to my van and drove over to the morgue.

I was told that Joe was busy cutting into a body and I could just go to administration and sign the papers. I found the office and the friendly girl got the paperwork out and I signed as being his cousin, which was a half-truth, but they didn't care as long as I signed for him. I called Hannigan on my cell and told him to come get the body and he said he would have one of his men come to pick him up. I went back to the van and over to Metro.

I was coming in the back hallway and ran into Captain Weber, not a person that I would want to talk to. He was really harmless, but to me he was so lacking in interest as to cause mental weariness.

"Richards, are you here to help with a case?" he asked.

"I'm still investigating the death of Ricky Lawless for his wife and you have two suspects in for questioning, I'm just observing."

"Well I hope it helps you as it will help us, we are so backed up with cases, I may start hiring you to work with us," he laughed and toddled off.

I found my way to Lynn's office and she was working at her computer. It was strange to not see Deacon sitting next to her, but he was in Vice now and probably off harassing hookers. Lynn looked up and smiled, which was a good sign.

"Thank you for spilling the beans to Deacon?" she said.

"Uh, what beans?"

"Don't play dumb, Penny told you I was pregnant and you let it sort of slip to Deacon that I had something on my mind. He bugged me all last night until I told him. It's out now so I don't have to worry about him driving me crazy. He's been real nice and gentle with me now, I think I like it."

"I'm glad it worked out then, how are you feeling about it all?"

"I'm mixed, but I'm happy about it, although it will be a burden on my job, I may have to change my life around a bit. Now I can get Deacon to finally commit to marriage," she said with a happy laugh.

"We got Lacey and Mac married, then Val and Blake last month, now it's time for you guys to hook up legally. We need another wedding to celebrate."

Trapper and Buffy came up to the door and he said, "Wedding? Who's getting married?"

"We're going to get Deacon to propose to Lynn and hitch them up," I said.

"As long as I've known Deacon, he's never said much about the subject of marriage. I don't even remember him having a girlfriend when he worked for me back in Michigan. We all wondered about him, hell even his sister said once she thought he was gay."

Lynn laughed and said, "You can believe he's not gay. I know that for a fact. Now, changing the subject, are you ready to watch my superb technique in interrogation?"

We all went to the observation room and stood looking at Buster through the magic mirror, squirming in his chair. Lynn checked the equipment to record the interrogation and said she was ready. She went out and to the room where Buster jumped when she came flying in through the door.

"Good morning Buster, I hope you are comfortable."

"Hell no, I'm not crazy about being questioned again and again about this. I told you everything I know."

"We just need to firm up a few things, and then we'll leave you alone."

"Well I hope so, I'm sorry Ricky's dead, but I don't know anything about how he died."

"Good, now I'd like to start at the beginning, the night Ricky died he came on stage with a glass of water, correct?"

"Nope, Linda brought him the glass and he set it on the stool behind him like he always did."

"Okay so Linda actually brought him the glass," she said as she scribbled some notes on the pad before her. "Did he drink from it right away or after his first song?"

"I don't remember if it was before or after the song, but he always drank to clear his throat. I have to state that I believe it was Linda who poisoned him. That's why she's running."

*

Chapter 20

"We don't know if she's running yet, and why don't you think Mary Lou poisoned him?"

"Mary Lou wasn't there, so it had to be Linda, she brought him the glass."

"Do you know what happened to the glass after Ricky died?"

"I wasn't watching it; I was concerned for my friend. Anyone could have taken it off the stool."

"So it wasn't on the stool after Ricky fell?"

"I don't know, as I said I wasn't watching it."

"Well, someone took it; CSI said there was no glass on any stool."

"As I said, I wasn't watching it."

"Okay, how many songs would you say were performed before he collapsed?"

"He was just starting the song 'I Wouldn't Want A Man Like That'. Our fourth song on the list."

Honky Tonk Murders

"So figuring about four minutes to each song, sixteen minutes; and about one extra minute between songs. So it was almost twenty minutes from when you started playing until he died?"

"Yeah, I guess you could say that."

"I talked to Joe Lang, the Medical Examiner, and he said that the concentrate of Potassium Chloride in the drink should have only taken about two minutes to kill a man of Ricky's size. So Ricky didn't drink for over three songs, then he finally took a drink. Long time for him to go without refreshing his throat, wouldn't you say?"

He sat quietly thinking, "Yeah, that would be strange, I'm sure he had to have drank from the glass long before that. I don't have an answer."

"Was anyone on stage besides you, Geech and the steel guitar player, who by the way we can't find."

"No one was on the stage but us. The steel guitar player, Scruffy Jackson, is on tour with another band now, that's why we had to move his equipment in Linda's van. No one else was on stage, why?"

"Because I'm thinking that someone switched out his glass or dumped in the potash to kill him."

"Well none of us did and no one was on stage, so you got a mystery."

"Or I've got three suspects who aren't talking. I'd like you to sit here quietly while I go talk to Geech and see what he has to say."

Buster didn't say anything, so Lynn got up and started to go out.

"Geech don't know nothin', he's a damn fine drummer but his brain is a bit fried. Too many drugs and drinking in his youth. He still nips a bit too much, but he can keep time with the music. He's harmless but not bright, that's why I have to watch over him. Please don't be too rough on him."

Lynn stood at the door, as the man took a sad look on his face, as if the world was handing him a bad deal. Lynn slowly came back and sat down.

"I had a feeling he was a little slow. How long have you been taking care of him?"

"Almost six years, he's thirty-two and never did much with his life other than play drums and party. Too much partying. We hooked up in a country band that lasted about five years and I had to watch over him. He's harmless, not much upstairs if you know what I mean.

"He's harmless, so he could never kill Ricky?"

"That's right lady, Geech would never kill anyone, he loves everyone. Please be gentle with him."

Lynn smiled and stood, "I'll be gentle, thanks." Then she went out and came into observation.

"What do you think?" she asked Trapper and me.

Trapper spoke first, "I think you should take him in the back room and beat him until he confesses."

"Lots of help, Will," Lynn said and looked to me.

"At this point you are not going to solve this unless someone confesses. There was no video recorded was there?" I said.

"I'm not hearing from anyone that there was. Hold on." She turned and went back to the room. Buster looked surprised that she was back so soon.

"Buster did you have any fans that liked to video record your band?" she asked him.

He looked like he was thinking on it. "There was one girl who had a crush on Ricky, I think her name was Gabby, short for Gabrielle. Yeah, that's her name, I don't know the last name. She was always recording us with her cell phone, and then she'd put it up on Youtube. You think she may have recorded the murder?"

"It's a possibility; I'll get back with you," she said and went out. By this time I was standing outside of observation and she came to over to me.

"You heard? Okay geeky boy, can you find the video online?"

"I figured you ask, get me to a computer." She walked past me and went to her office. Trapper and Buffy followed us.

Lynn pointed to her computer and said, "Go to it, do your magic."

I sat and brought up the browser on her computer and punched a few keys until Youtube came up. Then I did a search on Ricky's name and found a dozen videos featuring him.

"Looks like he was popular, these show recordings go back over six months. Here's three from Shindigs, one says it was Ricky's last performance," I said as I clicked it to play. Everyone was hovering behind me watching.

I put the video on full screen and we watched. "This video is fifteen minutes long," I said looking at the time listed on the video controls. "It starts from the beginning of the set."

Bob Moats

Lynn pulled her extra chair over and sat next to me watching. Trapper and Buffy stood quietly behind us. The camera work was real poor, but considering it came from a cell phone, we couldn't expect much.

"Can you go to the last five minutes where Ricky had to have drank the poison?" Buffy asked, starling me, I had forgot she was behind me.

"No, it's streaming video so we just have to wait as it loads. I have a program on my home computer that will download this, so we can study it later," I answered.

We waited; the video was going back and forth on the band and then out to the audience. It finally came back to the stage and then we could see someone on the stage behind Ricky and standing by his stool. The video resolution was crappy, to use a technical term and the person was wearing dark clothes. It was not certain if it was a man or woman, everyone wears jeans now days and longer hair. The person had their back to the audience and then went off the screen as the video recording moved away from the band and started showing the people at Gabby's table; everyone was waving and laughing. The camera went back to the band and the person was gone.

"Damn, we just saw our killer, now why didn't Buster remember that?" Lynn asked.

"I was following him on the video, he was busy watching his hands to see what he was playing, he must not be able to play without looking at his finger picking. I have to look at the keys on my computer keyboard when I type, total concentration on the keys or I can't type. Penny loves to sneak up on me when I type," I answered.

"Okay if you can get the download of this video, I'll send it to electronic forensic to see what they can pull off it," Lynn said.

"Why don't you bring Buster in and let him see this, it may rattle his brain to remember," Buffy said. We all looked to her, she just said, "What?"

"That's good Buffy, you may make a great investigator yet," Trapper laughed.

Lynn stood and went to the door and out. About two minutes later, she came back with Buster and sat him in the chair I was using. I started the video again as he sat and watched.

"Is this the video of Ricky's death?" he asked.

"Yes it is, now please watch and I'll tell you what to see, shortly," Lynn said to him.

We watched again and then it got to the place where the killer was on stage. The person came from nowhere to behind Ricky. It was dark and the lights flared the camera occasionally but the killer was there.

I paused the video and said to Buster, "You see the dark blob behind Ricky, that had to be the person who switched the drinking glass or dumped in the poison, you don't remember that?"

He leaned closer to the computer screen and squinted. "I see the person, but I don't remember them. I have a problem focusing myself, when I play."

"You have to watch what you are strumming on the guitar don't you?" I asked.

"Yes, I'm not very good at getting my brain to

work on what I'm doing unless I watch myself. It's something I had to do for years."

"So you don't remember anyone on the stage, but you can see that there was someone," I said.

He sat watching the screen, paused on the person who killed Ricky.

"Son of a bitch, right there and I didn't see. Man if I could tell you, I would," he said sadly.

"Well this takes the focus off of you and if I'm correct, Linda likes to wear short skirts, so that wasn't her either," I said leaning over to Buster. "Now was there anyone else who hung around that dressed like that?"

He sat thinking again; I presumed that his brain was not much better than Geech's, so we gave him the moment.

"Yeah, that reminds me of Jerry, the guy who replaced Ricky, he always wore dark clothes when he was our roadie."

*

Chapter 21

I looked over to Lynn, she just said, "I sent men to pick up Jerry, he wasn't in his motel room. They're watching for him." She leaned down to Buster and continued, "Buster, you can go get Geech and leave, I don't think we need to bother you now, but stay handy just in case we may need your help."

He thanked her and Lynn told the uniform

standing outside the door to take him and Geech and drive them back to their motel. Buster left with the cop and Lynn sat back at her desk, "How do you get this video to finish showing the murder?"

I reached over to the mouse and clicked the play button on the video, as we watched the band doing their last number. We watched Ricky collapse and then everyone rushed to him, everyone except the person in black. The camera work suddenly went screwy, I figured Gabby was startled by the scene and wasn't concentrating on recording. She didn't turn it off though, even if the footage was all over the room.

The video ended and it popped up a window asking if we wanted to replay. I shut it off. "I'll download it at home or you can explain to forensics where it's at and I'm sure they can. Now what?"

"We have to find Jerry, that's all we can do for now." She looked to Buffy and said, "Well, you saw the killer and based on what Buster said, it looks like Jerry had killed Ricky, possibly to get him out of the way so he could take over the band. We won't know until we find him, but the only singing he's going to do now is confessing. Looks like the band is finished."

I wondered what Buster and Geech would do now without the front singer. They couldn't play unless either of them could sing, they'd have to find someone else to replace Jerry. I've seen it happen one time before back in Michigan. I knew a band that had a front singer who was a terrible lush and frequently would fall off the stage drunk. They finally fired him and found a replacement fast, it can be done.

"Well this has been a productive morning," I joked.

Trapper turned to Buffy and said, "Like to go get lunch, ever try a Sonic burger?"

"I've heard about them but never had one," she replied.

"Good, let's go." He held his arm out and Buffy took it, they went to the door just as Lynn's phone rang. On instinct, Trapper paused. Lynn answered and listened a moment then hung up.

She turned to us and said, "They found Linda."

"Dead?" I asked.

"No, but she was tied up and held captive in a motel room, guess who's?"

Trapper grinned and said, "Our missing killer Jerry?"

"Spot on, Shamus. The men I had watching decided to do a little creative investigating and invented just cause to enter his room. They found Linda alive, but hog-tied on the bed. She wasn't happy with Jerry when they cut her loose."

"Are they bringing her in?" Buffy asked.

"They're on their way." She looked to Trapper, "How about some vending machine food instead?"

Trapper laughed and said, "If you're paying."

We all went to the break room and got snacks to last us for a while. I called Penny to see if she was done with her show, and she said she was. I filled her in on what was going on, she laughed and said Buffy won the bet, she took Jerry. We finished and I hung up.

"Buffy, you won the bet for who was the murderer if this pans out," I said.

She smiled and replied, "I hope I win both the bet and the report back to my home office. This will annoy the hell out of a few men."

Lynn's cell phone rang and after she answered, she said Linda was in the house. We all stood and headed back towards her office. "I had them put her in interrogation room 3, so we can go question her."

I was thinking this was hopefully going to be sewed up, and I could give Jenny some closure. Lynn led us to the observation room and we could see Linda pacing the room on the other side of the glass. Lynn checked the recording equipment and gave us a salute, went out to see Linda.

She entered the room and Linda went ballistic.

"Were the hell is that bastard Jerry! I hope you have him by the balls, because if you don't I will."

"Linda, please sit, I'm sure you've been through a bad time, take a breath, relax and tell me what happened."

Linda paced with her arms folded across her and then stopped. She threw her hands up in the air, pulled out the chair at the desk, and sat.

"Okay what do you want to know; I was kidnapped and held against my will by that psycho little shit, made to endure listening to his bullshit bragging about his plan to take over for Ricky."

"Why did he grab you?"

She was quiet for a moment then said, "I was talking to him after his set the other night, he was drunk enough to talk about how he had wanted to take Ricky's place for a while. He just sounded like he might know about Ricky's murder. He invited me back to his motel room, I was stupid to go but I wanted to find out what he knew about the killing, I wanted Ricky's murderer caught. Okay, I'm a little braver than I should be, but if I could get him to talk, it would solve your case. We went back to his room and he pulled a gun and then tied me up."

"We appreciate what you went through, but you could have been killed. Did he say if he murdered Mary Lou?"

"No, he never mentioned her. He just bragged about how he was taking over for Ricky and he would take over his song list. He didn't come right out and say it but he must know the recording company Ricky worked for. He said that the recording company was going to give him the contract that Ricky had."

In observation, I smiled and said to myself, "The plot thickens."

Lynn continued, "Did he admit that he murdered Ricky?"

"Actually he didn't say he did. He just was talking about how he was waiting for the recording company to contact him."

"So what was his reason for tying you up?"

She looked a little embarrassed and cleared her throat. "He admitted he wasn't very good with women, so he apologized for tying me up and having his way with me."

"Linda, he never admitted to murdering Ricky and he just wanted some rough sex with you, he's a bastard and pervert but he may not be a murderer. I would really liked to have you tell me he confessed, I'm glad you were honest, but this doesn't solve anything other than he is a kidnapper and sexual deviant.

"Well find him and beat it out of him," Linda said.

"I like this girl," Trapper said next to me.

"Linda we have video of the night Ricky died, it shows a person in dark clothes on stage by Ricky's drink, he had to be the murderer and Buster has tentatively identified him as Jerry. What do you know about that?"

She was quiet for a moment and sucked on her lower lip for bit, then said, "Jerry was on stage with the band, it was his job to check the equipment and refresh the drinks they would need. He was the roadie and he took his job seriously. The night Ricky died, Jerry was on and off the stage. I wasn't watching him closely but he was there. He could have poisoned Ricky's drink."

"But he never bragged to you that he did?"

"No, but he may not have wanted to implicate himself as the killer. Maybe he figured I would tell you what he said and that would get him off if you suspected him. Couldn't that be possible?"

"Very possible, but we will find him and we will get to the truth. So, you can go home to clean up, after you fill out some paperwork so we can pick him up for kidnapping, rape and false imprisonment. I'm sorry for what you had to go through, I hope you can get back to normalcy."

"Thank you Lieutenant Carter, I appreciate that. I wish he had confessed to me, but he did seem like he was holding back. Maybe he didn't want to confess, then he'd probably would have to kill me too." Linda visibly shivered when she said that.

"You may be very lucky, take care and if you remember anything call me," she said and handed Linda her card. Lynn stood and told the officer at the door to take her home after she filed a complaint.

Lynn came back to us, "We can't go on meeting like this," she joked. "I'm still for Jerry doing the murder. He was being cautious in front of Linda from what I could see. I don't think he wanted to kill her, so he just told her enough to satisfy his ego. I have more men watching his place, he'd have to come back to see if Linda is all right. When he shows, we'll get him."

"That's comforting, it's good your men found her first," Trapper said.

"Yep, we still aren't real close to closing this; I wish we had a better video of the murder. Maybe forensics can pull something more off the video we have. One can only hope."

*

Chapter 22

"You do realize that Jerry would have had to kill off Linda and dump the body, or face going to jail for kidnapping," I said. "He wouldn't want to risk his new recording contract by being arrested."

"Yeah, that thought came to me when I was talking to her," Lynn replied.

"If he was crazy enough or stupid enough to grab Linda, then he probably did in Ricky and maybe Mary Lou," Trapper said.

"Well, we just need Jerry, so it's all conjecture for now. Linda didn't give us what we wanted, a confession. Just when you think you got a good lead, we get sucked back into the mystery," Lynn said with a sigh.

"I'm going to find Penny and go get a real meal, that machine crap is not satisfying. Call me if you find Jerry," I said then turned to Trapper, "You two be good now." I laughed and left.

Out in the van I pulled my cell phone and called my lovely wife, she answered after the first ring. "Where are you now?" I asked.

"I just arrived at your office, I'm talking to Lacey, why?"

"I was wondering if you wanted to go get something to eat?"

"It too late for lunch and too early for dinner. But

if we fill up now we won't need dinner. I'm game."

"I'll pick you up in ten minutes or less."

"Or it's free," she said with a laugh.

"What, you think I'm paying for this?"

"It's your idea, so yes, you pay."

I hung up, no use in debating the issue, she always won. Or I'd be cut off from sex for a couple days. I drove out to my office and pulled into the front parking. I went in and found Penny holding Willy, still talking to Lacey. She smiled and gave me a kiss. I ruffled Willy's head and he tried to lick my hand, I let him.

"Has it been quiet today, I hope?" I said to Lacey.

"Yep, I put Jessie in the back conference room with her Gameboy, keeps her from being underfoot of everyone."

"I'm going to say hi to her," Penny said and went off, I followed.

As I passed Buck's office I saw he wasn't there, probably out checking his guards. I knew Trapper wouldn't be in, he was out checking Buffy. Earl was sitting at his desk on the phone, probably doing some investigating. About thirty percent of investigating seems to be on the phone, calling in favors and checking facts. He waved as I stood at his door, then went down to the conference room and found Penny standing next to Jessie. I came up and saw that Jessie had a book on the table in front of her, she was holding Willy in her arms. The Gameboy sat off to the side of the table.

"What are you reading?" I asked hoping it was one of my books.

Honky Tonk Murders

"A really scary book, about aliens trying to take over the earth, but there are nothing left but zombies on earth now and the aliens can't kill them," she said with a smile.

I tried not to laugh out loud, "Does Lacey know what you're reading?"

"No and you better not tell her."

"I won't, just don't have nightmares."

We talked briefly, then I said we had to go. Penny asked me, "Is it alright if we take Jessie to eat?"

Jessie looked confused, I said, "Yes Jessie we want to eat you, you didn't know we're zombies did you?"

"Stop that, you're not zombies!" she said with trepidation.

"No Jessie, don't listen to him. Jim and I would like to take you to a late lunch, would you like that?

"Sure, can I hold on to Willy?"

"Yes you can, now go tell Lacey."

She went out and we followed. We went to Carl's Jr and got take out, Penny had the table set up and we ate in the air conditioning of the van. I turned on some music low and we sat eating while Jessie told us about her school. Willy was running around the van and I put a small burger down for him. It probably would upset his stomach, but it kept him happy for now.

We finished up and relaxed, just as my cell phone rang. The caller ID said it was Hannigan Mortuary. I excused myself, went forward to the front of the van and sat in the driver's seat then answered.

"Mr. Richards? This is Beth from Hannigan's and Mr. Hannigan needs you to come in to sign some papers that authorize us to cremate Mr. Lawless, since you are not going through a funeral home. Can you stop by?"

"Sure, I can be there in about an hour, if that's alright?"

"That will be fine." We disconnected the call and I went back to tell Penny.

"I think we should drop Jessie back and go there, not a good place to take a young girl," Penny said.

"Why can't I go?" Jessie protested.

"It's a mortuary, they have dead bodies there and maybe a few zombies," I said.

"Jim! Quit that. Jessie, it's not a place for children, adults only, when you get older you'll understand."

"Okay, can I keep Willy with me?"

"Sure, I think he'd like that, we can pick him up later," I said.

We took her back to the office and dropped her off, then over to the mortuary. We went in the front entrance and found Beth at her desk.

"Mr. Richards, I saw you pull up and called Mr. Hannigan. He's in his office, go right in."

We went into Hannigan's office and found him behind his desk.

"Last time I saw you, you were up to your elbows in a dead body," I said.

"Perils of the business. Sorry to bring you in but this wasn't arranged through a funeral home so there has to be approval for our cremation from a relative, preferably a spouse but in her absence, Penny can sign."

"No problem, let's get this done quickly."

He put the papers in front of us, Penny signed on the dotted lines and we shook hands. Hannigan said the remains would be ready to be picked up tomorrow, just to call ahead. We finished up and went back to the van.

"That was creepy, having to give permission to burn a person," Penny said.

"He's not a person, it's a lifeless body. If we didn't get him cremated, the body would be a bit rank in a day or two."

"True, you take control of the urn, I'm not much for being around dead things," she said.

"Yet you hang around me," I said with a smile.

"You're only dead from the neck up," she responded.

"True." I started the van and drove out of the lot.

We went back and picked up Willy just before Lacey was closing up the office. Jessie gave us hugs and kisses and they went off. Buck came through the hallway from the back and gave us his walrus smile.

"How's you two doing?" the big guy asked.

"Good, we've had a busy day and now going home to crash. What have you been up to?" I asked.

"I was out scouting more places to guard. We're going to be the biggest security guard service in Nevada," he said with pride.

"Don't overextend yourself. I don't want to have to commit you. Have you talked to Angelo?"

"Yep, I gave him the week off starting this

weekend. I have one small job for him up till then."

"Make sure you put a bonus in his pay, so he can enjoy his trip."

"I already told Lacey to include it."

"Good, shall we go?" I said to Penny.

We were plopped down on the couch watching the Tivo recording of a couple shows we missed. I had put a small cooler next to the couch that had our beer in it, this really made us lazy now. The shows ended and we went to bed after sharing a nice warm shower. Willy was already asleep on his Bate's Motel chair as we slipped under the new silk sheets Penny bought on our last attack on the mall.

"You think it was Jerry?" Penny asked me.

"So far it does look like him. The video shows someone who looked like him on stage, just before Ricky died. Lynn said the poison should have only taken about two minutes to kill, and the person was on stage just before Ricky collapsed. I have to go with him for now but that doesn't mean it could change."

"Poor Linda, being tied up and mistreated like that. I hope Jerry is caught for her sake."

"Lynn's people are watching for him closely now. So we need to sleep, you have your show tomorrow and I have to go pick up the urn. Hopefully they will have Jerry in custody and we can get this finished up."

Penny kissed my nose and turned on her side, the one she turned to when she was going to sleep. I just cuddled and let her go off to sleep. I laid there as always thinking too much.

I must have drifted off quickly, I was suddenly feeling a chill and found I was on the bed in my underwear with no sheets on me. Penny thinks it's funny to pull them off to wake me. I rolled on my back and looked up at the ceiling.

"You are one mean woman," I said as I saw her pass through from her bathroom to the closet.

"But I still love you," she said with a smile.

*

Chapter 23

I was up and on the road, just after Penny had left with Willy. We didn't see our breakfast chef, Angelo, so I presumed he was working on Buck's short job before Angelo could go on his vacation. So I had made my toast, Penny cooked her oatmeal, and we were happy.

I drove to the office and parked, went in the back door, waving to the camera and stopped at Earl's door. He was standing at his makeshift crime board.

"Your case is that big you need a crime board?" I asked.

"Hell no, this is my fantasy football league. I have to keep track and this board works well," he said with a laugh.

"I don't even want to know," was all I said and walked further down the hall. I stopped at Trapper's office but he wasn't in. I figured where he may be, but I hate to suppose anything. Buck was on the phone probably arranging new businesses to guard. I continued to the lobby where I found Lacey concentrating on some papers on her desk. I knew if I stood still long enough she would suddenly see me and jump out of her skin. I had that effect on her. I decided to go quietly to my office, leaving her hard at work.

I sat at my desk and pulled the computer keyboard closer to me. I opened up a browser, went to Google and typed Phoenix Recording Studios, the company that was making Ricky's CDs. I hit enter and there were three references to the company. I clicked on the main website and read about their accomplishments and who the people were who ran the company. I copied off a few pages for future reference and read a couple more sites about them. I found a forum for people who were burned by recording companies and Phoenix was mentioned a few times, mostly about double dealing royalty payments to artists. Sounded familiar.

I shut down the browser just as Lacey came to the door. "About time you got to work," she said.

"I didn't want to scare you when I was standing out in the lobby while you were pouring over your paperwork, so I came back here quietly."

"I'm glad you didn't jump at me, I'm a little stressed this morning."

"Oh, what's wrong?"

"Nothing you want to know about women's problems, but I'd advise being careful with me today," she said and went back toward the lobby.

Women's problems? I knew that phrase, so best to avoid Lacey today. She could be real testy when she wasn't suffering from women's problems, so it was a code red when she was.

Buck came to my door, "Just wanted to warn you about Lacey…"

"Yes, I already got the hint, thanks. How's business doing?"

"Fantastic, I can't keep up with the companies calling now for guards. Vegas is a great place for us."

"As long as the money keeps coming in, I'm happy. Where did you send Angelo off to?"

"He's protecting a young, beautiful country singer, in town for some music benefit being put on by the Rio Hotel. Her name is Karisa Nowak, from out of Nashville. A few of the biggies that stayed after the CMA award show are hanging around for the thing also. It's just today and tomorrow, so Angelo will be free to go on vacation by the weekend. It's for a good cause, literacy for children, they give books to schools. The benefit is to raise money and awareness. Are you going? You're an author."

"I hadn't heard about it, get me some info and maybe I'll try to make it. Thanks."

"You got it, talk later," he said and went off. I picked up my desk phone and punched the button to dial Lynn, she came on after a couple rings.

"What now, Sherlock?" she said.

"Just calling to see if there's any progress on Jerry."

"Nothing so far, we're still watching for him."

"He never went back to check on Linda?"

"No, he probably thought she would just die there."

"It still makes no sense, then he would be wanted for Linda's murder, he had to have a plan to save his bacon."

"Until we find him it's all guess work."

"Yep, I have to go get Ricky's ashes today so call if anything comes up."

"His ashes? What are you going to do with them?"

"Do you pay attention to what I say? We're taking him back to Arizona to his wife this weekend."

"Oh yeah, I remember that now, I was happy to hear you were leaving town."

"Yes, but we're coming back, thank you."

"A person can dream," she said with a laugh and hung up.

I called Hannigan Mortuary and was told that Ricky was ready to be picked up. I went back out to the lobby and told Lacey I was leaving. She mumbled something sounding like "It's about time." I ignored her and went out to the van.

I arrived at the building and in to greet Beth again. She smiled and said, "Mr. Richards, go right in, Mr. Hannigan is waiting."

I entered the office and found Hannigan standing by a bookshelf. He removed the urn Penny had picked out and brought it to the desk. He picked up a fancy white cardboard box, just big enough for the urn. "Jim glad to see you, Mr. Lawless is all ready to go. Thank you for your patronage, the death business has been a little slow lately."

"Well, I'll see if I can stir up a few bodies for you," I said with a laugh.

"As long as you don't murder them." He handed me the box, it was fairly heavy for the size. I had never met Ricky or even seen a picture of him, so I assumed he was on the heavy side.

"Thanks again, now I can take him back to his wife." We finished and I went back out to the van. I opened the side door and put him on the floor next to the bathroom.

I got in and headed back to the office. On the way my cell phone rang and I saw it was Buck, I answered on the hands free. "Hey big guy, what's up?"

"I got you an appearance at the benefit if you want it. I talked to the person in charge and lied about being your manager; she was all excited about having you come by to help. You have to do this now."

I laughed and said, "Okay, call her back and find out what I need to do."

"I already got all the info, so when you came back I'll go over it with you," he said and hung up.

I had to laugh at Buck's enthusiasm, he always thought about others before himself.

At a stop light I looked back to Ricky's box and was a bit shocked to see it was gone. I pulled into a nearby parking lot and jumped out of the driver seat. I looked to the back of the van where the bedroom was and saw the box under the bed. I guessed it slid back there during my journey. I was just a little spooked that it had gotten back there. I pulled it out and took it back up and used the seat belt of the rear passenger seat to strap it down. Okay Ricky, get out of that.

I continued on to the office and parked, locking up the van so Ricky couldn't escape. Buck was in his office, "Hey Jimmy, those book people were more than happy to have you appear."

"I'm such a celebrity, it's hard not to love me," I said with a smile.

Buck spent about a half hour going over the information about my appearing at the benefit. Then I stood and said I was going to my office to call Penny. I thanked him and said, "Since you arranged all this you are going with me." He agreed.

I got hold of Penny and told her I had Ricky.

"You can leave him in the van until we take him to Arizona. I don't want him in the house," she said.

"I can put him in the garage until then, would that work for you?"

"Okay, that's close enough. Now what are you doing?"

"Waiting for Lynn to call to tell me they have Jerry. Otherwise nothing; why do you want a little sex?"

"Ha! Dream on, stud. I want some food. I think we can go to Arturo's for some pasta. Pick me up… wait, do you have Ricky in the van?"

"Yes I do, why?"

"I'll come by and we'll go in my car," she said and hung up. She totally amazed me. I presume she doesn't like dead people. I hope she never was in a zombie attack.

I sat in my office, Lacey came by once to drop off

some bills to be signed. Being the principle owner of the business, my signature was usually the one Lacey had on the checks for bills. I had put her on to be authorized to sign, but I wasn't going to question her today. I was busy putting my signature on the checks when Penny walked in.

"Lacey is having her time of the month?" she asked casually.

"What makes you think that?"

"She's a little tense, I figured as much. Some women are terrors during that time, Lacey is just tense. So shall we go eat?"

We slipped out of the building avoiding Lacey and went to Arturo's. On the way my cell phone rang, it was Lynn.

"I hope you got Jerry."

"Almost, he came back to the motel and had a gun battle with my men, he got away."

*

Chapter 24

"Can't you guys hold on to anyone?" I asked Lynn.

"Can you do better? At least we know he's still in town. We got BOLO's out and they did see what car he was driving, so it's a matter of time."

"Well, I'm going to be busy today, I've been asked to help promote literacy at a benefit in the Rio Hotel along with a number of country stars."

"Why? You're illiterate, who would want you to be in a benefit? You need a benefit for yourself."

"I'm a world famous author and the benefit is for books in schools. Good reason to participate."

"Okay, have fun and don't frighten any country stars," Lynn laughed and hung up.

"I'm surrounded by jokers," I said to myself. "And they aren't even funny."

"So we're going to a benefit at the Rio?" Penny asked from the passenger seat.

"Yes, I forgot to mention it, Buck set it up and I just have to make an appearance to promote books for school libraries. I think it is a worthwhile cause."

"Sure, if it includes your books. Are you donating anything to the cause?"

"I'll give a check for it. You know I like giving out money."

"Fine, just as long as you leave enough for me when you're gone."

"I'm going somewhere?"

"Sooner than later, if you don't get some food in me."

We pulled into Arturo's parking and let the valet take the van. We had a pleasant meal and then went out to drive to the Rio where I was supposed to meet with some woman named Lizzy Parker. She was in charge of entertainment. I guess I was entertainment, at least to my wife. We arrived and parked, they had the festivities set up in the back parking, where there was a stage being used by some country singer I didn't recognize. There were probably a couple thousand people milling around the area and we made our way to the stage where I saw Buck standing, talking to a rather attractive woman.

"Hey Jimmy, you made it," Buck yelled to me as we approached. "This is Lizzy Parker, she's the boss lady here."

Lizzy had her hand out and I took it, we shook, her hand was nice and warm. I didn't linger too long holding her hand with Penny eagle eyeing me.

"Nice to meet you Mr. Richards. I'm so glad you could come and help our cause," she said with a slight southern accent.

"Please call me Jim, and I'm glad I can help. What do you want me to do?"

"Well, if you could just give a short speech about the importance of books in school libraries and do a little begging for donations, it would help."

"I can do that," I said with a smile.

Lizzy looked to Penny, "We'd be honored if you could say a few words too, Mrs. Wickens."

"Off camera it's Wickens-Richards," Penny said, "I'd be happy to help. My husband and I can do this together, can't we Sweetie?"

What could I say, "Sure, that works for me."

Lizzy beamed and said, "Great, I'll let you know when you can go up on stage." She walked off to go up and introduce the next performer, Karisa Nowak. I heard that name before and realized it was Angelo's client. I looked around for Angelo and saw him next to the stage where a very cute, young looking blonde was going up to sing. I told Penny I was going to talk to Angelo and she nodded. Angelo gave me a big smile as I approached and said, "Hey Mr. R., hows

154

you doing?"

"Good Angelo, how's the client?"

"She's a real peach, real nice, I like her. After this I take her for a sightsee around Vegas, she'll like that."

"I'm sure she will, just don't get in any trouble," I said thinking back when Angelo and the porn star were kidnapped during the Hypnotic Murders.

"I'm keeping a better eye out for trouble now, no more trouble for me."

"Good, hang around for a bit to hear Penny and I give our speech on stage."

"I'll do that."

We said our good-byes and I went back to Penny. We stood listening to the girl singing, she had a very distinctive voice, cute and bubbly. She finished her two songs then Lizzy introduced Penny and me. We went up the steps to the stage to fairly good applause, probably more for Penny than me, she was more well known. I gave a quick spiel about how books are needed in schools, and to donate to the cause. Then Penny told about her experiences with authors on her show and how important books were.

We finished about ten minutes later and left the stage so they could bring up another band. Buck came over and said, "Good promotion, guys. I was listening to the comments in the crowd, you guys rocked."

"Better than being stoned," I said. Penny poked my ribs. We stood listening to the next band just as I was looking around the crowd. There were all types of people watching, some in cowboy hats, some in baseball caps. I saw one man on the other side of the stage in a dark ball cap that had the Arizona Diamondbacks baseball team logo on it. I looked down to his face and was shocked to see it was Jerry.

I turned to Penny and said, "Call Lynn now, Jerry is here. I'm going to go see if I can detain him." I told Buck to follow me; Penny said to be careful as she pulled her cellphone.

Buck and I went around the back of the crowd and along to the side where Jerry was standing. I quickly explained who Jerry was since Buck hadn't gone with us on this case. We came up fairly close as I pointed him out to Buck. I put my hand on my Glock under my jacket but didn't pull it, in this crowd a gun may start a panic or half of the cowboys would pull theirs and start shooting. I waited until I was up close. Buck came up on my right and whispered that he would run interference for me. Jerry was just grooving on the music, I thought this was too easy.

I came up close behind him and had my Glock in his back and said quietly, "Jerry don't move or you won't like what I'll do."

Buck came up on his right and stood close. Jerry turned to look at Buck who was glaring at him. I poked a little harder and said to move out of the crowd. He went to his right with Buck still close, moving people out of the way, as we went to the edge of the crowd towards the parking lot.

Just as we came out of the crowd, three young girls got in our way and Jerry reached for the closest and grabbed her, swinging her and him around with the girl between him and my gun. Buck now had his .38 out and we both had him in our sights, but didn't want to hurt the girl. From somewhere, somehow, Jerry had a smaller .38 in his hand and had it on the girl. I remember Lynn saying Jerry was in a shootout with the cops.

Buck moved over to his right so Jerry was now almost between us. He started to yell, "Stop moving or I'll kill her!"

The crowd behind us now saw what was going on and they started screaming and moving away, which was good.

"Come on Jerry use some brains, you kill her and you're dead. I'll be very happy to plug you good and Buck loves to shoot people," I said hoping he'd had enough smarts to realize it was futile. His back was to a fence closing off the benefit from the parking, so he couldn't go very far. I was hoping Lynn would get here quickly.

I heard movement to my left and saw Penny come up with her .38 out. We had Jerry flanked on three sides, nowhere for him to go now. I knew Penny was such an expert shot, I wondered if she would do something. I just worried that Penny might get hurt. Buck went close to the fence on Jerry's left, facing us. Jerry put the gun to the girl's head and screamed for all of us to get back. The girl started struggling and opened Jerry up on Penny's side, she fired. Jerry screamed in pain as his arm went limp dropping his gun as the girl ran off.

Buck and I went to Jerry, grabbed onto him, forcing him to the ground. He was bleeding from his right arm where Penny shot him. I picked up Jerry's gun and slipped it into my jacket pocket then I pulled my cell phone and speed dialed Lynn explaining to her that we needed an EMS.

The crowd was now reforming around us as Buck was yelling to keep back. Hotel security came charging up and I explained to them the situation just as Lynn and Detective Warren ran up. Lynn badged the rent-a-cops and smiled at the sight of Jerry on the ground. EMS pulled into to the area as the hotel security opened up the side fence gate. The med techs put Jerry on a gurney as they worked on his wound. It was superficial, but effective, my wife knows how to shoot. We explained the situation and Lynn sent Warren with Jerry to the hospital after warning him to keep a close eye on Jerry. Warren handcuffed him to the gurney and said, "No problem". They went off as Lynn came back to us.

"This certainly helps now that we have him, you did good girl," she said to Penny.

Penny smiled and said, "All in a day's work for Richards' Investigations."

*

Chapter 25

"Of course you will have to be questioned by our people as to the shooting, but I'll go to bat for you," Lynn said to Penny.

"Bring them on, I shot in good conscience," she laughed. "Bastard bureaucracy."

Lynn laughed even harder. "You go girl."

"Can we go now?" I asked. "I mean if you aren't going to be able to interrogate Jerry until they release him from the hospital."

"Are you in a rush to go somewhere?" Lynn asked.

"I had a big meal before coming here, and I see there is a long line for the port-a-potties. I need to go back to my van and use the facilities."

"I wouldn't use a port-a-potty if you paid me," Lynn said. "Go, I have no use for you now. I'll call when we have him in interrogation, which according to the paramedic may be later today."

"Fine, I'll see you later. Buck, keep an eye on Penny while I rush to my van," I said and took off. I could hear Buck's loud laugh and Penny yelling something about abandonment. I wasn't interested at the moment.

I had finished my business; it was nice having a bathroom traveling with you. I could even shower if I felt like it. I was closing up the van when I saw Penny and Buck coming towards me.

"Get tired of the festival?" I asked.

"Too many people and music's too loud and it's too damn hot out, yes I'm tired of it," Penny said. "Now fire up the air conditioning in the van and head home where I can swim."

I turned to Buck, "Are you going back to the office?"

"Hell no, Lacey's still on her rampage, I lay low once a month for her," he said with a smile.

"You're more than welcome to join us, what's Maria up to?"

"She's sleeping probably, it's a bitch when you're a showgirl and have to work late. That's why I like working the night shift with the guards. We get to sleep together that way."

"You get to sleep with the guards?" I said with a smile. Buck just shook his head and walked to his car.

I got in the van, Penny was already in her seat, started it and put the air on. I drove out to our home nestled in the hills on the west side of Vegas. It was always so peaceful and quiet out there, other than when Penny was way out in the back doing target practice with her gun by the hills. I would join her occasionally, just to keep my firing hand steady. Our nearest neighbors were a good two city blocks away and they never seemed to be upset when they heard shooting. Although the man who lived there did come down one day to find out if someone was killing people. After that they left us alone.

I pulled into the drive and parked; Penny jumped out and headed for the door. I knew she'd be in the pool before I even got into the house. She usually just dropped her clothes on the way to the back and swam naked, which I didn't mind.

Willy was bouncing around the kitchen as I came in; he was most likely hungry. I poured a bowl of his kibble and he attacked it with glee. I could hear the water in the pool splashing, so Penny had made it safely.

Bob Moats

I went to my home office and sat at my desk. I could see Penny swimming around in the pool through my back window; she looked so scrumptious with her naked body all wet. I turned to my laptop and fired it up. I opened up the latest book I was writing about the Talk Show Murders back in Michigan and spent some time adding a new chapter as I listen to Penny talking to Willy after I opened my window.

About an hour later my cell phone rang and the caller ID said it was Lynn. "Hey flatfoot, what's up, did you beat a confession out of Jerry yet?"

"Nope, I was hoping you'd come in and do that to save me from a lot of internal affair's questioning. What are you doing?"

"Just sitting here, working on my next book, hoping to make more money. Is Jerry in the precinct yet?"

"Yes, he is and since Penny brought him down, I'm letting you know that you can come in to listen to me beat the truth out of him."

"Penny is wet right now, give us about an hour and we'll be in. Have you called Buffy at all, this case hangs in a balance for her?"

"I called her first and she and Trapper are on their way."

"Trapper is still escorting her?"

"I think they're getting married. Poor girl," Lynn said with a big laugh and hung up.

I leaned out the back window and yelled to Penny that it was time to go question Jerry. She bounced up and yelled to give her a couple minutes. I knew she could be ready in a flash so I closed down my laptop after saving and backing up my book files. I've lost too many files in the past so now I backed up everything to an external hard drive and a USB drive.

I went out to the van and Penny came bouncing out a few minutes later holding Willy.

"We're taking the pup?" I asked.

"He needs to know we still love him."

"Of course," I said and drove out.

We drove into Metro, parked and went into the back door, up to the desk guard who by now knew better than stop us. He hit the desk button to unlock the new door to prevent bad guys from getting in or getting out and we entered.

Captain Weber was standing by the door talking to an officer in dress blues. He looked over and excused himself from the man, coming to us as we walked down the hall.

"Penny, would you like a job in Metro?" he said with a big grin. I figured he heard about the shooting today.

"I'm happy where I'm at thank you," Penny replied.

"Well, we don't condone citizens shooting up people, but between you and I, good job." He smiled and walked off.

"That man has little to say doesn't he?" Penny said.

"Yes, which is good, now let's go find Lynn."

We walked through the squad room and found Lynn standing talking to Deacon. Trapper and Buffy were with them.

"Hey big guy, how's Vice?" I asked Deacon.

Lynn said, "Don't even answer that." Deacon closed his mouth and winked to me.

Lynn took all of us to observation and we stood looking at Jerry through the glass.

"His wound was not enough to cause problems but was enough to stop him. Good work Penny."

Penny whispered to me, "I was shooting to kill, but my aim was off." I chuckled and gave her a kiss on the cheek.

"You're aim is never off, babe," I said.

Lynn said it was time, set the recording equipment and went out of the room to Jerry's side. He flinched when she entered and Lynn sat quickly.

"You've been read your rights, this conversation is being recorded, you all right with that…" then she whispered to him, "Don't say no, you don't want problems."

He said out loud, "I got nothing to hide and want to give my statement, I didn't do anything wrong. I was helping with catching the killer of Ricky."

I was wondering what he was talking about, this would be interesting.

"He's going to lie through his teeth," Trapper said.

Lynn opened the file she had in front of her, usually she had nothing but paper in it, to just shake up the suspect. She studied the papers then closed the file. "Okay Jerry you have a statement to make?"

"I didn't kill Ricky, it was Linda," he said with a defiance. "She put the poison in his drink and made me take it to Ricky. I didn't know it was poisoned until after, when I found out that's what had happened to Ricky. She never told me, just said to take it to Ricky's stool; his glass was almost empty. So I did, it was part of my job. I was the only person allowed to go on the stage."

"Okay so you're saying that Linda handed you a glass of water and told you to give it to Ricky. How long before Ricky died did this happen?"

"It was just before the last song he sang when he died. He thanked me for bringing him the glass and picked it up and drank from it. If only I knew, I wouldn't have let him drink, I liked Ricky, he was good to me."

"How can you be sure it was Linda who poisoned the drink?"

"Well, she gave it to me and it was the glass they say poisoned him. So it had to be her."

"Why didn't you tell us this earlier?"

"Are you kidding, I was involved in the murder, I didn't want to go to jail. I just kept my mouth shut like I didn't know anything."

"Why did you tie up Linda in the motel and leave her?"

"Okay, I invited her back to my motel to find out if I could get her to talk about the murder. The bitch pulled a gun on me and I managed to get it from her. That's when I tied her up and tried to get her to talk, but she wouldn't. She just did a lot of swearing at me. I had to get out and think, so I left her there. I came back and found the cops there, I panicked and used Linda's gun to get away, I was stupid. Am I going to jail?"

Lynn smiled and said, "I think it's a good bet."

*

Chapter 26

Lynn stood and excused herself, she went out to the squad room and I could see through our window that she was talking to Warren. He got on the phone and made a call; I figured it was for a warrant to arrest Linda. Lynn came back to us.

"Well, any opinions?" she said when she came in.

"It's possible, I mean he seems too stupid to make it up," I said.

"My thoughts too," Lynn agreed. "I had Warren put out an arrest warrant for her. Now we wait again, I'm hating this."

"What about Mary Lou?" Trapper asked.

Lynn thought about it for a moment and went out of the room. She re-entered interrogation and sat.

"Jerry, talk to me about Mary Lou."

"What? She was threatening Linda to go to the police about the murder. Linda told me she had no idea how she found out, but Linda said that Mary Lou slipped her a note saying that she knew what she did and wanted to meet her at the parking structure. I got the same note before Mary Lou was killed, but I was told to go to a different parking structure. I assumed Mary Lou handed out a couple notes to see who would show up, to get the killer out in the open. She found the right killer, Linda, and she got murdered."

Now I had to think that the note they found in Mary Lou's pocket was one of a few she gave out to different people. Poor Mary Lou was just trying to find the killer of her husband.

"Did Linda admit to you that she killed Mary Lou?"

"She implied it, but never admitted it. I tried to get it out of her, but she never admitted it."

"Did you meet with Mary Lou at the parking structure she told you to meet at?"

"No, she was already dead by then."

"How did you know this?"

"She didn't show up so I went back to the bar and later heard she was dead."

"Jerry we have you for murder, kidnapping, false imprisonment and rape…"

"Rape!! I never raped that bitch! She wouldn't do anything but fight me, I almost had to knock her out she was so violent. I never raped her. No kidnapping either, I just tied her up to get her to talk. I was holding her for the police. So I didn't kidnap her, it was a citizen's arrest!" Jerry was panicking now and fighting against the handcuffs that held him to the table.

Lynn just sat back and watched him; the boy was definitely manic now. "Jerry, who else did Mary Lou give notes to?"

"How should I know, I only found out that Linda got a note when she told me, I just figured she sent them to everyone."

"Who gave you the note? Marry Lou?"

"I found it under the windshield wiper on my car, the same place Linda found hers."

"Jerry, we have a warrant out for Linda, when we get her back here I hope your stories jive."

"She'll lie to you, I know she will, I didn't know about the poison in Ricky's drink, she tricked me."

"Will you take a lie-detector to back up that statement?"

"You bet I will, I'm innocent!"

"Jerry you should have come to us earlier, you could have avoided a lot of grief for everyone."

"I know, but I wanted to be sure, I wasn't thinking right."

"I doubt he has enough brains to think at all," Trapper said sitting next to me in observation, it got a laugh from Buffy. I could see the two of them together; they both had a weird sense of humor.

Lynn stood and went to the door, calling for the uniform to come in and take Jerry to his cell until she could arrange for the lie detector test. She went back to Warren and talked to him. He got on the phone again as Lynn headed to observation.

"Well, it's a waiting game again," Lynn said as she entered the room and plopped down on the now empty chair after Deacon got up for her. "Anyone have a good impression, and nothing from you Will," she said with a smile to Trapper.

"You can kid about it, but I was the one who said Linda did it," Trapper said.

"Both of them have small holes in what they are saying, maybe once we have Linda, I can play them

167

against each other. We'll see," Lynn sighed and sat back.

The door opened and Warren poked his head in and said, "Lynn, officers at Linda's home say it was vacant, as in she's fled the place. I put a BOLO out and updated the warrant to include flight risk." He went back out.

"I'd say the girl is worried now," I said and looked to Buffy. "Do you have enough evidence now to rule out a plot by the beneficiary?"

"I think it's safe to say, but I don't want to report too soon, then I'd have to leave Vegas," she said with a grin to Trapper.

"Well don't take too long, Ricky's wife could use the money," Penny piped in.

"I know, I'm just kidding, I'll be putting in my report by tomorrow after I fill out the forms. She should have a check by next week."

"I'll let her know," Penny said.

"We can tell her in person, I'm thinking of taking Ricky's remains out sooner, if you can get a couple days off from your show?" I asked Penny.

"I think I can, when do you want to go?"

"We can start tomorrow afternoon, just get the van packed with essentials and plot our course."

"What if we catch Linda?" Lynn asked.

"You can stream the interrogation to my laptop; I'll watch it on the road. Right now I'm not caring, I just want to get out of town and all this craziness," I said.

"Wow, the world famous P.I. has given up. Is the end of the world far behind?" Lynn laughed.

"Nope, just taking a breather and wanting to travel, my van is calling," I replied.

"You do the cooking on the road, so it's alright with me," Penny added.

"I love the smell of cooking on the road. Shall we take Angelo with us to be our chef?"

"I think he'd do better than you."

"Well, do what you want, I need to catch Linda and solve this case," Lynn said.

"We'll send you postcards from the road," I said and stood, "Come my dear, let's go get ready to take Ricky home."

"Where are you putting him?" she asked.

"In the lower storage if it will make you feel better."

"I like that," she said as she stood gathering up Willy who she tied to the leg of her chair. We said good-bye to everyone and left the room. We got to the van and Penny asked, "Where is Ricky now?"

"In the garage at home, I didn't want someone to steal the van and make off with Ricky. Jenny wouldn't like that."

"I'm confused," Penny said suddenly.

"Aren't you usually?" I replied.

She whacked my arm and said, "No doofus, you told me what Linda said and now I watched as Jerry talked, their stories conflicted so much, one is a real liar, or they both are."

"I think they are both covering their asses and making it all up. You're right, nothing makes sense. But that is Lynn's worry now, we are taking a vacation. Do we need anything at the store?"

"I need a new swimsuit," she said with a grin.

"Hell you do, you already have a couple hundred, but we do need some food supplies, shall we go to the grocery outlet and stock up."

"I'm game," she said and sat back.

We went shopping at different stores and stocked up. I finally steered the van back towards home and we went into the house. Penny went to feed Willy and I brought some of the items from the van so we could arrange them for storage in the compartments in the van. I looked over and Penny was gone, I figured she was changing into the new swimsuit she bought at the store. I couldn't stop her, it was a fixation for her to have a swimsuit for everyday of the year, including winter.

I saw her breeze through the dining room to the sliding doors out back, she was in the pool before I left the house to follow her. I stood watching her and looked to Willy. "Shall we go pack the van?"

I went back in the house followed by the dog singing to myself about going on a road trip, and got everything together for packing.

About two hours later, after nuking convenience food for dinner, we sat in our favorite spot, the couch. We had our beer and chips, with dip this time and watched TV for a while.

I suddenly turned the sound down and handed penny my cell phone.

"What?" she asked.

"You said you were going to tell Jenny that we were coming out and what has happened so far."

"Oh, right." She took the phone; I reached over

and pushed a speed dial button. Penny put it on speakerphone, and after six rings, Jenny came on.

"Hello, Jenny?" Penny said. Jenny acknowledged and then Penny continued by telling her who she was and gave her the rundown on our case and of our upcoming trip out to Phoenix. My beautiful wife was efficient.

Jenny was quiet and then said, "I got a call about an hour ago from some person saying he murdered Ricky and that he was sorry."

*

Chapter 27

I took the phone from Penny, "Do you have caller ID?" I asked.

"Yes, but it was blocked. The person called and just said he killed Ricky and he was sorry but it had to be. That was all he said, then hung up."

"I suppose you didn't recognize the voice, did it have an accent?"

"Well, it was someone who was country born, but sounded like they were disguising their voice so I couldn't say if it was anyone I knew. Jim, what's going on?"

"I wish I could tell you, the case is still ongoing but as Penny told you we are taking some time and bringing Ricky back to you. Have you arranged with the funeral home for a crypt?"

Honky Tonk Murders

"It's all arranged, yes. I'll give you more details when you get here."

"Okay, sit tight and don't let this new development get to you." We said our good-byes and hung up.

I dialed Lynn and when she came on I said, "Got a new development for you. Has Jerry used any phones in the last hour?"

"No, he's not even asking for a lawyer. He says he's innocent and the lie-detector test says he may be telling the truth. What's the new development?"

"We called Jenny in Phoenix and she said she got a call from a male voice saying he murdered Ricky and he was sorry for doing it."

"Crap, this is getting deep, did she know who called?"

"Nope, she didn't even get the number from caller ID, it was blocked."

"Can you get hold of your buddy Harold in the FBI and see if he can get a trace on the call?"

"I was thinking that, I'll try and see if he can find out where the call came from. At least it wasn't a female voice, so maybe Linda didn't have much to do with it."

"I'm still going to haul her in and question her. Let me know if your friend can find out something."

"I'll call you later," I said and hung up. I dialed Harold, it was probably after midnight in Washington, but I had to act quickly. He came on sounding sleepy and I told him who I was.

He didn't say anything right away but I finally heard him say shit. "Come on Harold, be nice, I just need a small favor."

"You always need a small favor, what's the crime now?"

I explained everything from the beginning, then told him about the phone call to Jenny.

"You want a trace on the number, right?"

"If you can, I don't have the pull you do."

"I'm only doing this because I'm a fan of country music, I'll see what I can do, give me the number." I gave it to him and he hung up without saying good-bye. At least, he didn't swear again, that was good.

I looked to Penny and Willy sitting next to me. "The mystery continues, but I'm not worrying about it for now, I want to enjoy our trip."

We packed it in for the night, I wanted to get an early start in the morning. I had planned out the route, it would take us off the main highways and freeways and we'd have a nice scenic drive through the mountains of Arizona. It would probably take an extra day to get there that way but I wanted to camp at least one night before we got to Jenny's.

Penny was sound asleep by the time I finished the last details of planning. I laid on the bed thinking about the new developments in the case and wondering why would someone called Jenny and confessed to murdering Ricky. He could have called the police and confessed, it would save a whole lot of trouble for us. I guess the killer didn't really want to suffer the consequences but felt guilty enough to apologize for his crime. Great, a murderer with a conscience.

I had drifted off a short time later when my cell phone rang. I reached over in the dark and knocked it off of the bed stand. I had to fumble around on the floor trying to find it, them my hand felt it and brought it up quickly.

"Hello," I said as I looked to the digital clock on the small table, four a.m. it said.

"Did I wake you, Jim?" came the voice of Harold. "Sorry if I did, but now you know how it feels." He let out a chuckle and continued. "I got a number for you."

""Where did it come from?"

"Vegas of course, but the number goes to a cell phone, one of those cheep ones you can buy in any gas station or drug store, so there's no hope we can get a name. Probably in the trash by now, too." He read the number, I wrote it down on the pad of paper I kept on the table.

"Thanks for that, I'll pass it to my friends in LVMPD and let them worry about it, now you can go back to bed."

"Bed? It's seven a.m. out here in Washington, time to go to work. "All us good little black ops must protect the country no matter what time it is." He laughed and hung up.

Penny rolled over and asked, "Well?"

"The call came from Vegas, so we still have a killer in town. I'm glad we'll be out of town."

"You're going to desert your friends in this time of crisis?"

"You better believe it, I'm tired of saving the world."

Penny rolled over laughing, "Saving the world, you can't even save your own butt."

I didn't argue, I just tried to go back to sleep.

Around eight a.m. I called Lynn and gave her the news and the number. She said she'd see what she could come up with. I knew it would be useless, but this did bring up the fact that Jerry and Linda both didn't do it. Someone out there is thumbing his nose. Or could someone be trying to divert our attentions away from Jerry or Linda, and why? That would mean there was a third person involved. My head hurt, so I got my brain into the trip.

Everything was loaded in the van, Penny and Willy got in and I drove out. I got almost to the end of the drive and stopped.

"What? Penny asked.

"Never mind," I said and jumped out of the van. I came back a number of minutes later and put the box with Ricky's remains in the back.

"You forgot Ricky?" Penny laughed.

"No, I remembered, just a little late. Now drop it." I put the van in gear and headed out.

"Did you get Angelo all set up for his trip?" Penny asked, thankfully changing the subject of forgotten bodies.

"I told him we would probably be back before he left, but if not, to just go. He'll make sure the house is secure. We should be back before Sunday; he's planning on leaving Monday morning."

I had put my new Palm LifeDrive in the holder on the dash and set the GPS to guide us to the border of Arizona and beyond. It should take us a couple hours to get to Kingman and then due east on US-40 to Flagstaff where we would head off the main roads and down through what I hoped would be the scenic drive to Phoenix.

We headed down 95 into Boulder City and cut over to 93, that would take us to Kingman, Arizona. From there we caught US-40 across to Flagstaff. I wanted to avoid the big cities and the traffic, so I plotted a course around most of the busy areas. I didn't mind driving as long as the scenery was pleasant, and I liked the rocky mountain area along the way.

I drove on for about six hours and finally found our campground; Payson Campground & RV Resort on East State Highway 260, nearby Payson, Arizona. We pulled in and Penny jumped out to stretch her lovely legs. Willy was bouncing around her, until she picked him up. I swear that dog was getting lazy, he had been carried too much.

I went in to register and pick a site to pull the van into. We found the plot and parked, set up camp and sat on their picnic table to relax. I took a big breath and kissed Penny on her cheek.

"Want to go with me to buy some firewood?" I asked her.

"Nope, I'm not into manual labor, I'll sit here with Willy keeping an eye on the van and Ricky's remains," she said.

"Good idea, I'll be right back." I kissed her again and went to the office where they had a huge stack of firewood at ridiculous prices, I bought two bundles. I lugged them back to our site and put them next to the firepit. Private campgrounds and RV parks were nice, but I usually liked to go camp in the national forest campgrounds where it was primitive and peaceful. Unfortunately, most national forest campgrounds were now overrun by strange people trying to save a few bucks. I paid more for this place and expected to get a little luxury.

As it started to get dark I put the firepit together stacking the wood perfectly. I knew how to build a fire. I got it started and we sat watching the flames lick towards the sky and Penny sighed, "This is so relaxing."

"Yep, I love camping," I said as my cell phone buzzed.

"You answer that and I'll murder you," Penny threatened.

I looked at the caller ID, it was Lynn. "Sorry babe, got to take it." I answered saying hello.

"Jim, we got another death, this time it was Buster."

*

Chapter 28

"You don't have Linda yet?" I asked.

"No and she's eluding our every efforts."

"How did it happen?"

"According to Joe Lang, it's the same type of throat cut that killed Mary Lou."

"Where was he murdered?"

"He was in the bar tearing down their equipment, they had no front singer so the band was told to leave and a replacement band was going to come in."

"Anyone in the bar helping him?"

"The bartender said no. The bar was closed and she was setting up the back bar with new stock, it was just Buster and her. She went to the basement to hook up a new CO_2 fountain container, and when she came back up a half hour later, Buster was prone on the dance floor, bleeding out and dead."

"Where was Geech?"

"The bartender said that Buster told her he was back at the motel, sleeping off a drunk. We sent a car to the motel and Geech was there, looking very bad. He's now here being held for questioning. Paul from CSI said the blood splatter showed that Buster was attacked from the rear and the person had to be tall to have brought the blade around his neck to cut. That rules out Linda, she's a lot shorter than Buster was."

"So it's a whole new suspect, and you have nothing to go on," I said

"Thanks for reminding me, hey this was supposed to be your case too," Lynn protested.

"And I'm on the case; I'm delivering the victim home. But I'll hurry back to solve this for you."

I hung up as she started to swear at me. I looked to Penny and she frowned. "Let's not let this ruin our vacation."

"What could ruin this perfect night?" I said as Penny stood. "Where are you off to?"

She smiled and went into the van, coming back out a few minutes later carrying a bag of marshmallows. "Babe, I hate marshmallows," I said.

"I know; these are for me. She pulled a long stick from the box on the picnic table that had our cooking gear in it. She had a good time roasting the marshmallows and shared a couple with Willy after they cooled.

We spent the rest of the evening sitting quietly by the fire. After we used all the firewood and the fire finally died down, we went into the van to close it up for the night. I flipped on my laptop, hooked up the wireless broadband adapter and checked my email. There were no nasty notes from either Lacey or Lynn, so I closed it down. We went to the bedroom and crawled into bed, deciding to just get some sleep. It was quiet and peaceful the rest of the night.

I woke early and went out to get some fresh air. Willy was doing his business, which I cleaned up after he finished. Penny came staggering out and smiled at me. "Did you sleep well?" she asked.

"Yes, very well, you?"

"Same, I even had nice dreams with no murders or being kidnapped. I think we need to get away more often."

"I agree, but innocent people need me to solve their crimes."

"There are enough police out there to do the job and you're getting old," she said with a grin.

"Hey, you're only two years younger!"

"But I'm young at heart."

"And in body. I'd say you could pass for a forty year old."

"Forty, hell. I could pass for twenty-nine."

I wasn't going to continue this line of sure death for me, so I just started picking up the gear around the van and putting it away. About an hour later, we were on our way again heading into Payson to get gas.

I found a self-serve station, pulled in and up to the pumps. Penny said something about snacks and jumped out of the van. She was heading towards the building that said food mart on the side. I looked to the pump and it had a sign asking patrons to pay first. I followed Penny to the building and noticed a Sheriff's vehicle parked on the side.

I entered the building and Penny was already hitting the snack racks. I went to the counter where the young female clerk was talking to a rather good-looking man in a clean, crisp Sheriff's uniform. He smiled and stood back, but I could tell he was eyeing me. I was wearing a jacket, and in this hot climate, that probably caught his attention. I wore it to cover my Glock in its holster, but my gun was presently locked in the console next to my seat in the van. I handed the clerk a fifty-dollar bill and said I needed a fill-up. She took one of those pens that revealed counterfeit money and check my bill, it passed.

I looked to the sheriff and smiled, "Good morning, Sheriff." Penny came up with an armload of snacks and dumped them on the counter.

I heard the sheriff say, "Morning folks, just passing through?"

"Yes sir, we're on our way to Phoenix taking the scenic route from Las Vegas. We have the remains of a murder victim that we're taking home."

He gave me an odd look as I continued, "Sorry, let me explain, I'm a private investigator in Vegas and the deceased is my wife's cousin's husband. He was murdered last week and we haven't caught the killer yet, but I have the victim's remains. He was cremated at the widow's request and we are driving his ashes to Phoenix for burial."

The sheriff smiled now, "You carrying?"

I pulled back my jacket to reveal the empty holster. "My Glock is locked away in the van, although I feel naked without it."

He laughed and said he understood. I glanced at his name badge over his pocket, it said N. Bracco. I smiled and said, "We just left the Payson Campground, now I have to drive into Phoenix. Never been there before, how are the roads in?"

"All good, just drive carefully."

The clerk had Penny's snacks all packed and I gave the girl a ten for the six dollar tab and said to keep the change, pointing to the tip jar by the register. She thanked me and I nodded to the Sheriff and said thanks.

We went back to the van, Penny got in and I pumped the gas. I drove the van back out to the main highway and headed towards Phoenix.

"That Sheriff seemed pleasant," Penny said.

"And tough, he was once the head of a terrorist task force that took down some big name bad guys who wanted to blow up the United States, his name is

Nick Bracco."

"And how do you know this?" she asked.

"I collect Law Enforcement Trading Cards," I said with a grin. "He was VIP of the FBI. I'll have to mention to Harold that I met him."

"You never cease to amaze me. You have a story for everything," she said and then laughed.

"Yes dear, I'm a fountain of information," I said.

"Mostly bullshit," she laughed.

"Hey, you're not allowed to swear."

She just looked out at the scenery and laughed.

We finally pulled into Phoenix passing through Scottsdale and a few other busy towns. I pulled in to a convenience store and pulled my cell phone, speed dialing Jenny. She came on after a few rings and I told her it was me.

"Jim. I'm so glad you're in town, I've been so frightened from the phone call."

"Well it wasn't a threat against you; it was an apology for murdering your husband, so I don't think you have anything to worry about."

"Maybe, but I want to get this over with, please. Do you have Ricky?"

"Yes we do and if you give me your address we'll be there shortly." I took my Palm LifeDrive out of the holder and typed in the address she gave me. I started the GPS back up and set the Palm to guide me to her home. We drove through Phoenix trying to avoid the traffic and finally found her home out in a rather spread out area. Ricky evidently did well with his recordings, the house looked like it was owned by a well off person.

Penny jumped out of the van holding Willy and went to the front door as Jenny came out. I went around the van, opened the side door and took Ricky's box from the seat that it was strapped in. I closed the door and took the box towards the house.

"Penny, it's so good to see you!" Jenny yelled as they hugged and did the women's happy dance. I wasn't going to do any happy dance with Ricky's remains.

Penny pulled Jenny to me and introduced us. "Jen, this is my husband, Jim Richards, Jim this is Jenny."

"Good to meet you considering the circumstances."

"Have you heard anything about the insurance money?"

I thought that was a strange question. She was more concerned about the money than her husband's remains. "I'm sure that the insurance investigator who is on the case is making a favorable report. But the call you received puts the case back a day or two. I didn't get much from my connections in the FBI as to who called you, just a number in Vegas. I also have to talk to you about a new murder, someone who you know."

"Please come in and we can talk." She led us into the house. We went into her living room and sat.

"You said there was another murder? Who?"

"Buster Jones."

Jenny had a shocked look on her face then broke down and cried loudly.

*

Chapter 29

Penny was trying to comfort Jenny as I sat there wondering why Jenny took Buster's death harder than her own husband's murder. The two women rocked back and forth for a few moments then Jenny gathered some strength and sat up.

"I'm sorry, Buster was a dear friend who I knew for years, long before even Ricky. It was me who introduced Buster to Ricky, when he was forming a band. Buster took the job and they worked to build up Ricky's recordings. It was actually Buster who wrote the songs Ricky sang, but Ricky was the front man and the singer, so Buster took a back seat to Ricky, letting him take credit for the music."

I wish I had talked more to Jenny when I had started this, but I was sure she wouldn't have shared this information if Buster hadn't been killed.

"Jenny you really have to talk to me, this is important, what do you know about Ricky's death?"

She sat rocking back and forth now, I thought she was going to cry again, but didn't. She was looking around the room, like she was either trying to find a way out or looking for someone.

"Jenny where is your daughter?' I asked.

"She's staying with a friend until after Ricky gets put in the crypt. I didn't want to subject her to this."

"Okay, good, now talk to me about Ricky."

She wiped her eyes with the tissue Penny handed to her and said, "Ricky was a pig! He was screwing around with women on the road and even married two so he could get their money."

I knew about Mary Lou, but a second wife? I didn't ask right now, I just let her talk.

"How did you know that Ricky was doing all these things?" I asked.

"Buster called me just about every other day and told me all the details. I had asked Buster to do this, he didn't want to at first but then Ricky was so out of control he didn't care.

"So you knew about Mary Lou and this other wife? Why didn't you do something about it?"

"I didn't want to lose the money for my daughter, she was so sick and needed lots of treatments. I figured if I divorced Ricky he wouldn't take care of us, the bastard. I knew if I were still married to him, it would be harder for him to ignore us. Plus if I threatened him with the bigamy he would have to take care of us."

"Did you threaten him with it?"

"No, I held my tongue and played the good wife, as long as he was doing well with his records, I was able to take care of our daughter. I knew I could use the bigamy threat if ever tried to screw us. That was all I cared about, fuck Ricky."

I didn't know what to say, but asked, "Jenny do you know who killed Ricky?"

She was quiet for a moment then said, "Last night Buster called me and…" She started to break up again, Penny hugged her and said to be strong, she

185

sat back up and continued, "Buster was crying and said he was the one who poisoned Ricky's drink. He was apologizing so much I didn't know what to say, then Buster said that the insurance would take care of us for a long time. I hate to admit it but that wasn't such a bad thing, even though Buster had murdered Ricky. I didn't know beforehand that he did it. I didn't know if I should turn him in or let it go. Now it doesn't matter. But, Jim, who killed Buster?"

"I'm not sure but I think I have an idea. Was Geech a good friend to you too?"

"Geech? Oh God, no. Geech was someone who Buster felt sorry for and took care of for a long time. The man was a waste of flesh, drunk all the time and stupid. I felt sorry for him but he wasn't a favorite of mine. Although he worshiped Ricky. It was Ricky who let Geech stay with the band because he was a good drummer. But off stage he was a degenerate. I knew that Geech had problems with the law years ago, but never knew what it was."

I thought about it, Geech was taller than Buster so he could have slit Buster's throat. I excused myself and went out to the hallway and pulled my cell phone. I speed dialed Lynn and waited. My call went to her voice mail, meaning she was busy questioning someone or at a crime scene shootout, she never ignored my calls. I left a message to hold on to Geech and call me back as soon as possible.

I went back to where the women were and picked up Ricky's box. "Here's his ashes, do with them what you will." I handed the box to her and she just stared at it. Then she removed the cover and took out the

186

fancy urn that Penny had picked out.

"Penny, did you pick this urn?"

"I did, I hope it's alright."

"Very nice, much better than he deserved." She stood with the urn and left the living room heading to the front door. Penny and I followed. She walked to the street and then went down a ways until she stopped over a sewer grate. She looked to us with a slight smile, then pulled the top and poured the ashes into the sewer. She closed the urn and handed it to Penny.

"Here, clean it out and resell it. I don't want it." She smiled and walked back to her house.

I was trying not to laugh at the irony, from the slime so goes to the slime. We followed her back and went in, just as my cell phone rang, it was Lynn.

"Hey, do you still have Geech in custody?" I nearly yelled.

"Hey, calm down. No, we talked to him; he says was passed out and remembers nothing. We let him go," she said.

"Crap, go get him, he's my bet for Buster's killer. It's a sordid affair, but I definitely know now that Buster killed Ricky, and it's looking like Geech killed Buster."

I heard Lynn move the phone away and called for Warren to go find Geech again. She came back on and said, "You better have a good explanation."

"I said I'd solve your case for you didn't I?"

"Don't pat yourself on the back too hard yet, talk to me."

I explained everything Jenny told us and I could hear her sigh then exhale. "You did good, we'll find Geech and get this straightened out."

I told her I would talk to her later and we hung up. I went back to the women and they were just sitting quietly, Penny was looking uncomfortable.

"I called Lynn and told her to find Geech. I think I'd like to get back to Vegas as soon as possible," I said.

"I can drive most of the way," Penny said with a smile as she stood. She turned to Jenny, "We have to get this finished before you can collect on your insurance. Nice to see you again but we have to go."

I was surprised to see Penny so excited about closing a case that I didn't question her. We left the house and back to the van.

"We're taking the freeways all the way back," she said.

"Fine with me," I said.

"I've had enough of scenic, I'm a big city girl."

We waved to Jenny and pulled away from the house and headed back.

We stopped at another gas station and Penny went in to get some Pepsi for both of us as I paid for the gas.

After I filled the tank again, I pulled over to the side of the station and checked the map, "We can take 60 up to 93, it's mostly minor roads but it will cut the trip in half and avoiding Flagstaff altogether. I'm surprised that you wanted to get back so quickly to catch Geech."

"I wasn't interested in catching Geech, that's your job. I realized sitting with Jenny just how much I didn't like her. When we were younger and I had to visit her family with my parents, she was a nut job. She whined about everything and had mood swings that scared me. I had forgotten all that until I was sitting with her and you were talking to Lynn. I had to get away."

I chuckled quietly thinking that there wasn't much that frightened Penny, I found one. We drove on the road and about half way home Penny said she'd drive. I had let her drive the van when we were coming across America on my book tour, so I knew she could handle it. I needed the rest anyway.

We made it through Kingman and then up towards Boulder City. We had less than two hours to get home as long as traffic was good. It was now close to three in the afternoon, it was a fast day. I pulled my cell phone since I hadn't heard from Lynn and called her.

"Any progress?" I asked when she came on.

"We're still looking, where are you?"

"About an hour away. We'll see you soon," I said and hung up. I sat back watching the scenery go by, it was nice having Penny drive. I was thinking about Geech, he wasn't a very bright bulb but one thing he loved and was good at was his drumming. I wondered if he had gathered his drum set yet. If he didn't think the police suspected him, he may have gone to get his equipment. But since the bar was a

189

crime scene, would he be able to get in? I waited until we were just outside Vegas before I called Lynn again.

"We're almost there, I had a thought, maybe Geech might be at the bar getting his drums?"

"Didn't even think of that, I'll go personally, meet you there," she said and hung up.

*

Chapter 30

I had taken over driving from Penny and was heading up Rainbow Boulevard towards Tropicana. I pulled into the parking lot and found Lynn's unmarked car and one black and white parked in the back. There were people standing outside the building, talking in small groups. I parked and went to a group of three and asked what was going on.

"There was an argument between some woman and a guy in the band, then the cops came in and the band guy grabbed the woman. They got a hostage situation. We were told to get out by the cops," the man said; I presumed they were customers.

I thanked him and went to the backdoor, stopped and told Penny, "It may be better if you stayed out here."

She opened her purse and pulled out her .38 and said, "I'm in this too." I wasn't going to stand and argue.

"Well just stay in the back until we know the situation." I went to the door and slowly pulled it open, looking in I saw down the hallway from the door, two officers with their guns drawn facing into the room where the stage stood. I couldn't see who they were training their weapons on.

I entered with Penny behind me, I had my Glock out and ready. We came down the hall and one of the cops looked back to us, he was the cop I knew as Tim. He nodded and when we came up, he said, "Careful, this guy is nuts."

"Does he have a gun?" I asked.

"No, he has a big carpet knife on some woman's throat and he's acting crazy. Lynn is trying to calm him down."

I went into the room and saw Lynn standing on the edge of the dance floor; Geech's drum set was all pulled apart and on the floor to be put in their cases. Geech was standing by the sidewall holding on to some woman from behind her. He had poking her throat one of those big curved knives they use for cutting carpets, sharp and deadly.

I came up slowly next to Lynn, she still had her gun on Geech, she saw me and said, "Welcome to the party. You're fashionably late."

"Got caught in traffic, I would have been here sooner. So what's the plan?"

"Wait it out and see what he demands."

"Have you asked him?"

"Hell, we just came in and after we saw that he grabbed the girl, we got everyone out. He just stands there; he hasn't said anything, even when I ask him what he wants. You got a better idea? This is getting boring."

I could see Geech had a crazy look in his eyes and was acting very panicky. I put my gun back in the holster and walked towards Geech slowly. Then he came to life.

"Get back or I'll cut her throat, I can do it you know, I did it to Buster and I caught Mary Lou by surprise, I can do it."

"Sure Geech, you could do it, but then all these officers would have to shoot you, that's not such a good idea. I saw Jenny today, Geech," I said hoping to distract him.

He suddenly looked surprised, "You did? How is she? She's not mad that I killed Buster is she? I had to, he killed Ricky, I loved Ricky, he was good to me. But I found out Buster killed him, so he had to die. And that LA bitch Ricky was married to, she sent me a note saying that I killed Ricky, I went to tell her I didn't but she kept threatening me, so I did her too and then put her in the van and dumped her in the trash where she belonged."

"Yep, you got rid of all the bad people didn't you, Geech? Now you have to stay alive, Geech. Why don't you put down the knife and let the girl go. Then we can all talk and get this straightened out."

"No, no talk, you cops will just shoot me, I know because I did bad things. That's what you do, you shoot bad people. I'm not bad, I did good by killing bad people, didn't I?"

"Yes, Geech I said you did good. It must have been hard to kill your friend, wasn't it?"

"He was mean to me, he threatened to tell the cops that I killed Ricky, but he told me he did, he put the poison in Ricky's drink after Jerry brought it up to the stage. He told me everything just before he went to the bar to get his equipment. I followed him in my car and confronted him here, we argued and he turned his back on me, so I cut him. I went back to the motel and hid until the cops came and took me in. I didn't tell them I knew about Buster. They let me go."

I could see Lynn was heading towards the front of the building and then crossed over to the same sidewall Geech was standing at. I move to my right to take his attention away from the front. I stayed the same distance from him, just pulled his attention around to face me. Lynn came up on the wall behind him; he couldn't see her while facing me.

I went to his drum set on the floor and leaned over to tap my fingers on the snare drum, it made it's rat-a-tat noise. Geech perked up. "Sounds good, Geech," I said as I kept tapping to hide any noise Lynn may make.

"Easy on my drums, they are my life," he said.

"I'm a fan of the drums, Geech. I know you are very good on them." I now had Geech turned between Lynn and me. I also knew that Lynn was well trained in hand-to-hand combat, I hoped she could disarm Geech without harm to the girl.

Honky Tonk Murders

I tapped harder, to distract him, "Hey easy there," he yelled. I just kept tapping as Lynn was only feet away. Just as she got up behind him, I started to pound on the bass drum. He really got upset and moved the knife away from the girl and pointed it at me screaming to stop that. This gave Lynn the moment she needed - she grabbed the man's wrist giving his arm a twist back and kicked out behind his knee cap - the man dropped. The girl ran towards me, I grabbed her and told Tim to take care of her.

I went to Lynn who already had her foot on his throat and was twisting his arm, taking the knife from him. The other patrol officer came running over and they spent a few seconds struggling to get cuffs on him as he was screaming.

Lynn stood, looked to me and smiled. "Okay, we make a good team."

"I need more money," I said.

"Talk to Weber," she said with a laugh. "Now we need to sit everyone down and get this mess straightened out."

An hour later Penny and I were sitting in the squad room by Warren's desk as Lynn had Jerry handcuffed by another desk. Geech was chained to the desk in interrogation where we could see him. He was upset, which I could understand. I felt sorry for the man, not very bright and murdered the only man who was agreeable to take care of him. Well, the prison system will take care of him now.

Lynn was taking notes from the new confessions that Jerry was giving, he admitted he lied about what happened with him and Linda. He thought Linda had provided the poison and was protecting his own ass. Lynn just shook her head and told Warren to take him back to his cell to be tried for kidnapping and false imprisonment of Linda. Jerry wasn't happy.

Lynn sat next to us. "We got Geech's statement about the whole thing; the DA is taking over now and will be getting him arraigned for murder. We still don't know where Linda is, I hope she's alive."

"She's probably down in Mexico by now worrying that she's wanted for murder," Penny said.

"By tomorrow the media will tell the story and maybe Linda will surface. I still need to clear up a few details with her," Lynn said.

"How's the baby doing? Any problems?" I asked Lynn to change the subject.

"I went to the doctor's the other day and they did some tests, the baby is doing good. I've got about seven more months they say. I'm just a little upset that Deacon and I will deliver a baby without legitimate parents."

"I think that will be taken care of soon," I said as I could see Deacon coming down the hall. He had called me earlier about what he was going to do. I told Penny and we both grinned as Deacon came up to Lynn.

She smiled up to him from her chair and then he got down on one knee and took out a small box, opening it and said, "Lynn for the last two plus years you have made me a happy man, I'd like to make it right for you, will you marry me?"

She looked in shock at the diamond ring in the box and actually broke down and cried. I had never really ever seen her cry. The squad room went nuts and everyone cheered.

Lynn kissed Deacon and said yes.

Penny leaned forward and said to Lynn, "We need to go see Shelby Francis." Referring to the wedding planner who did our wedding and then Val and Blake's wedding last month. Finally another wedding to celebrate.

Life was good.

*

Chapter 31

Two weeks later, the morning came early for us, Penny was rushing around the house getting into her Maid of Honor dress. I was already in my tux for being Deacon's best man. Today was the day, after all this time, they were finally getting married. I hoped for the right reasons, not just because of the baby.

Last night I threw a bachelor party for Deacon at a local strip club, with Lynn's blessing. We had just about all the off duty LVMPD cops in to celebrate including Captain Weber. It looked more like a police convention which made a number of customers in the club uneasy. We had a good time and no problems, Deacon was a good boy. Besides, Lynn would castrate him if he got out of line with the strippers and warned Warren to keep an eye on him. We survived the night with few problems or arrests.

Penny finally came out and said she was ready. We got in the van and went to the same chapel that Penny and I then Val and Blake were married in. I'm now sure that Shelby got a kick back for using that place. I went to the back of the chapel where Deacon waited nervously and he smiled when I came in. He handed me the rings and I wished him the best.

We stood waiting at the altar as Captain Weber escort Lynn down the aisle. He looked almost as happy as Lynn. She looked beautiful in the off-white wedding gown and they arrived for Weber to give Lynn away. Father Tom, who presided over our wedding and Val and Blake's wedding, stood at the altar and did his thing to join the happy couple in wedded bliss.

I looked around the room and saw Trapper with Buffy, she was relieved that the case was tied up and had made her report to the home office, which would make Jenny very happy. All of Lynn's detectives were sitting in the pews wanting to get to the reception and start drinking again after filling themselves at the bachelor party. Buck stood next to me in his tux for being in the wedding party. Deacon's sister Maria was a bride's maid and she was totally happy. I remember the first time Deacon met Lynn at the scene of a murder I was investigating, and Maria told me she worried about Deacon being gay, now she could relax.

The ceremony ended and they ran out in a shower of birdseed, at Penny's insistence, and I let them use my mini-limo being driven by Angelo. We met later at the MGM Grand for the reception, where the cops had a good time toasting and toasting Lynn and Deacon.

The celebrating ended, Lynn and Deacon ran off to go on their honeymoon, Penny and I bought them tickets to Hawaii and they left in the mini-limo after they changed clothes and their bags were packed in the car. Penny took charge of the wedding gown and I had Deacon's tux to return. We both went out to the van and drove home.

We entered in the house and settled in. Willy was bouncing around our feet as we plopped down on the couch.

"This was a very interesting case," I said. "Geech was arraigned for two counts of murder in the first; Jerry is going to get a suspended sentence for his testimony on the band. Unfortunately, Linda is still missing, I hope not dead and I need another vacation."

"How about we renew our wedding vows and go on a second honeymoon?" Penny asked.

"I'd like that, shall we start our honeymoon tonight." I grinned and she went to the bedroom, I followed.

*

THE END

For every end there is a new beginning.

Bob Moats

Read a preview of the next book "Dark Carnival Murders."

Chapter 1

They slowly moved in under cover of the pale moon. Enough light to see what they needed to do; but not enough to attract much attention. The convoy of trucks pulled into the center of the expansive twenty acres of still untouched desert land. In one corner of the property sat construction equipment and supplies to soon build the most expensive and most glamorous towers of condos in Las Vegas, but the work had been delayed while the investors battled over profit division.

The trucks came to a stop in formation for the building of another type of attraction; the men flowed out of the cabs and started to pull out equipment and parts to build the rides on which people would find thrills and chills.

A huge tent went up at the perimeter where the rides were being set up and a gaily colored banner was strung across the front of the tent where it could be seen easily from the road. It read "Jacob S. Dark's Traveling Carnival and Wonder Shows."

Three hours later, the tent was equipped with all that was needed to amaze and amuse the crowds with the greatest sideshow of geeks and freaks found on earth.

From the edge of the lot, two young boys were

watching the activities. They had told their parents that they were camping in the backyard in the pup tent they had set up. But the flyer they had found blowing in the street summoned them to the lot where a bigger tent and rides were growing before them. So when it was finally dark, they'd snuck out of the yard and walked the mile from their home to the place where they knew magic would happen. They quietly moved up to the back of the tent and listened carefully at the canvas.

Suddenly a flap in the tent opened and there stood a tall, dark man, in a black suit, the type a funeral director from the western movies would wear. Tall stovepipe hat, a pencil thin mustache and he had what the hip folks on the strip would call a soul patch beard.

The boys froze, one felt a trickle of wetness running down his leg, the other just made a small yelp. The man smiled and said loud and boisterously, "Welcome boys, don't be frightened, this is my carnival and you can come in to help set up the side shows and the games of chance. I pay well, and you get to go on the rides for free. Just step on in and I'll take care of you."

The older boy looked to the other and nodded, then they happily ran into the tent. The tall, dark man grinned, looked out to the vast area to see if anyone was watching, and then slowly closed the flap.

~~*~~

It was Saturday morning and I wanted to sleep in, so I had already warned my beautiful wife Penny not to disturb me under penalty of death. I, of course, couldn't sleep so I just stared at the ceiling as Willy, our tiny toy Yorkie licked my foot hanging over the edge of the bed. I usually slept in strange positions but my leg over the side of the bed was not one of them. Moreover, Willy's tongue tickling my foot wasn't on my list of favorite things.

I gave up and swung my other leg over the bed causing Willy to rush out of the room before I could trample him. I stood and stretched, went to my bathroom and started my day.

A half-hour later I came out to the kitchen, but it was empty. No Angelo, no Penny. Odd, I thought and saw the patio door was open. I went out and stopped by the ugly Greek God statue that still occupied the patio, reached down into the can at the foot of the statue and pulled a handful of feed, throwing it into the Koi pond in front of the statue. The huge goldfish devoured the pellets and I ventured on past them. I could smell food cooking and went to the backyard and found Angelo and Penny at the incinerator, which is what we called our BBQ.

"Smells great, what's cooking?" I asked.

"What are you doing up? I thought you wanted to get some sleep?" Penny asked.

"Willy kept waking me," I said with a grin.

She walked over and gave me a kiss, then said, "Sure, blame the pup. You just couldn't sleep in on such a beautiful day. Angelo decided to make breakfast burritos and he asked if he could cook on the grill for the meat, onions and peppers."

"Good morning Mr. R. I'll have these ready shortly," Angelo said as he was flipping the foods on the skillet.

"Thank you Angelo, it smells great." I turned my attention to Penny and continued, "I hope Lynn and Deacon are enjoying their honeymoon," I said, talking about our friends finally getting married a week ago, it was a good ceremony, then Penny and I sent them to Hawaii for their honeymoon. "I checked the online weather in Hawaii and they have no monsoons or volcanic activities."

"And as long as there are no murders, they should be happy," Penny offered as we sat on the picnic table watching Angelo do his magic with food.

"What are we planning on doing today?" I asked.

"I was reading in the Review-Journal that there was a carnival in town, I haven't been to one in years, shall we go there?" Penny said with a hopeful look.

I thought back to my hometown in Michigan and the carnival that would set up every year behind my parent's home. "I used to go help get the side show games set up when the carnival came to my town years ago. It was fun to be around and they would give me tickets to go on the rides free. I think it's a good idea."

"Good, because I already invited Angelo to go with us."

"Sure of yourself, eh? What if I said no?"

"I would have taken Angelo and went anyway." She stuck her tongue out and stood as Angelo said the food was ready.

We gathered our soft shells and spooned on the ingredients, rolling them to eat. "Angelo, you're Italian, where did you learn to make Mexican food?" I asked.

"When I was young, mom had a cook on the estate that was Mexican and she taught me," he said with a laugh.

"Your grandmother had a restaurant and taught you to cook, now you tell me you learned to make Mexican treats. You should open a restaurant and call it ItaliMex. It would be something different," I said.

"Angelo, how is Francis doing?" Penny asked.

"Mom still calls me every couple days. I miss her but I had to get away from the family life. Being a enforcer for the mob was not something I wanted to do all my life. I like it here and as we talked about, I may still open a restaurant."

"What about the bodyguard work you're doing for Buck?" I asked.

"I like that but I need something more creative, food has always been a passion of mine," he replied.

"Thankfully for us," Penny whispered to me.

"Yes dear, I'm very thankful you don't have to cook." She whacked my arm, I was getting used to it by now.

We finished our breakfast and went in to finish getting ready for the day. My cell phone buzzed and Penny gave me an evil eye.

"If that's a murder case, forget it," she said.

"The caller ID says it's Earl," I told Penny and answered it.

"What's up chief?" I said and put it on speaker phone.

"Just wanted to see what you guys are up to, we haven't gotten together very much since Paula and I have been out here," he said.

I looked to Penny and she said to me, "Ask them if they want to go to the carnival?"

Earl heard her and said, "Carnival? I love carnivals. Where is it?"

"Out south of the strip in the area where they are doing all the new construction. The property is still open desert land and the thing is being sponsored by some community group to give a good family spin on Vegas. Interested?" Penny said.

"Sure, shall we come meet you at your place?

I spoke, "No, go to the office, it's just up the road from where they are set up, we can meet there."

"Sounds good, how soon?"

"We're getting ready to go now, see you shortly," I said and hung up.

We gathered everything we would need to start our journey; Angelo met us in front by the van.

"Gee, Mrs. R. I haven't been to a carnival in years. Last time, we had to run out because the Feds were after my late father."

Penny was trying not to laugh, and got in the van and buckled up. We were all seated and I drove to the office on Industrial Road. It was about three miles from the desert area that would soon be a luxury complex of condos for the rich, now inhabited by the carnival.

I pulled into the parking lot of the office and saw Earl talking to a man and woman. I pulled in and parked. Earl waited until Penny, Angelo and I got up close, and then introduced the people.

"Jim, this is Mr. and Mrs. Walker, they just pulled in before you and they told me they have a problem."

The man came forward and held out his hand to shake, I took it. "Mr. Richards, we need your help. The police can't help us right now. Our boys are missing, they were supposed to be camping in our backyard, but early this morning we found they were gone. We don't know where they could have went to, but we found this in the tent." He handed me a folded yellow sheet of paper.

I opened the folded sheet and read the announcement about the carnival coming to town. I had a feeling this was going to be interesting.

*

Continued in the book...

~~*~~

Jim Richards Family of Readers

Thanks to the following people who are now part of the Jim Richards Family of Readers. They have read a book or more and enjoyed them. They all volunteered to be included in the list. If you are a fan of the books, send me your full name and you will be included in future books. Send your name to murdernovels@bobmoats.com to be added here and on the website.

* Achim Feifel * Al Norris * Alex Wheatley * Alexandra Delporte-Wilkinson * Amy Tapia * Andrea Bryan * Anne Shepherd * Arianda Sugar * Arlene Markowski * Ashley Augustus * Audra Hall * Barbara Hughes * Barbara Sammons * Barbara Schuler * Barbara Zirger * Beth Donohue Plenskofski * Betsy Childress * Beth Gibson * Bill Sandy * Bill Tornquist * Billie-jo Collie * Boni J Rychener * Carl Bishopric * Carla Lewis * Carole Henderson * Carolyn Conroy * Carolyn Riddle-Linington * Cassy Bailey * Cathie Turner * Chad Hudson * Charlotte L Duran * Cheryl L. Everett * Cindy Ackley Nunn * Cindy Valstad * Connie Bancroft * Corinne Kay O'Daniel * Dana Robbins Chuchran * Dana Wichita * Danielle Monique * Darren Heald * Dave Travers * David Wilkinson * DeAnn Jannereth * Deanna Miller * Deb Breuker Balbo * Debbie Carter * Debbie White * Deborah Fartuch * Deborah Gauze * Deborah Sullivan * Dee King * Denise Freeman * Diana Carver * Dixie Beck * Donna Gould * Donna Thompson * Donny Minter * Doris Kight

Bob Moats

* Eddie Moore * Eric Walters * Felicia Annette Bradfield * Francine Menor * Gail Chesney * Georgiann Minster * George Conner * Greg Colucci * Hayley Rankin * Harold Garcia * Heidi Arnold * Irma Ranee Coy * Jacqueline Moss * Jan Kimball * Janice Schneider * Janice Spoor * Jennifer Redmond * Jessica Keown-Belous * Jim Beck * Jo Boguslaw * Jo Turner * Joanne Marie Turner * John Peiffer * John Wisbiski * Joseph Wauro * Joyce Stacy * Joyce Trifiletti * Judy Franklin * Judy Travers * Judy Padgett * Julie Heath * Junnahvee Benson * Karen Dahl * Karen Grams * Karen Higham * Karen Kaiser * Karen Meinburg Richwine * Karen Kirkman Parker * Karin Hawkins * Karin Vasvari * Kathleen Donohue Roesing * Kathleen Riddle-Wolfe * Kathy Hinds Moore * Kathy Jones * Kathy Mitchell * Katie Benzler * Kay Burns * Kelly Garcia * Ken Boggs * Keota Rodriguez * Kiera Mccarthy * Kim Estes * Kitty Stolle * Kristie Sciler * Kirsty Stanton * LaLonnie Scallen * Larry Morris * Leann Parr * Lenora Scales * Leslie Marie Jackson * Linda Forester * Linda Ingle Cox * Linda Kennerö * Linda Magill * Lisa Bower * Liz Gibson * Lorraine Wiman * Loretta Alexander * Lynda Bowles * Lynette Lawrance * LuAnn Louttit * Manny Rothman * Marcia Gibson DeWitt * Marie Calder * Marlene Bryan * MaryLouise Kramp * Mary Lynn Gross * Megan Atkins * Meghan Hyden * Melody Cannavan * Michael Carruthers * Michael Dinkens * Michael Vannoy * Michelle Burns-Mitchell * Michelle Pilcher * Micki Potter * Mike Moats * Mimi Baur * Myrna Hecht * Nadine Sutton * Nancy Ellen Sayre * Natalie Quine * Neena Martin * O'Della Wilson * Pat Pollington * Pat Rohn * Patricia Jarmon * Patricia C Trezza * Patrick Barry * Paul Lawrance * Peggy Davis * Phyllis Bassett * Raylene Matheny * Rebecca Collins Besner * Renee Brumley * Reta Hanna * Reta Moats * Roberta Navarro-Harder * Sally Berneathy *

Honky Tonk Murders

Sally Hubler * Sarah Santos * Satka Nikc * Sharon E. Edwards * Sharon Mangini * Sharon McMillon * Sheena Rawl * Sherry Amstutz * Shirley Alvarez * Shirley Davies * Shirley Williams * Stacie Rowe * Stephanie Conner * Steve Cullen * Susan Haughton * Susan Hesse Adams * Susan Salomon * Suzan K Chase * Taisha Cullum * Tamara Moore * Tammy Castleberry * Tammy Lynn Wood * Ted Murphy * Terri Atkins * Terri Creech * Terry Raab * Tonia Rachael Riggs-Williams * Travis Fleury-Lopez * Twyla Gawlas * Val Brooks * Walt Munsel * Yvonne Isakson *

Thank you to all these wonderful people.

Thank you for purchasing this book. I hope you enjoy it as much as I enjoyed writing it for my faithful readers. Please feel free to email me to tell me what you thought about my stories. I love hearing from the readers. I can be reached at murdernovels@bobmoats.com thanks again!